TROGLODYTE

. . . . .

TROGLODYTE

■ ■ ■ ■ ■

Tracy DeBrincat

ELIXIR PRESS *Denver, Colorado*

PUBLISHED BY ELIXIR PRESS

P.O. Box 27029

Denver, Colorado 80227

Library of Congress Cataloging-in-Publication Data

DeBrincat, Tracy.

[Short stories. Selections]

Troglodyte : a short fiction collection / Tracy DeBrincat.

pages cm

ISBN 1-932418-48-2 (alk. paper)

I. Title.

PS3554.E17673T76 2014

813'.54—dc23

2013014567

Cover art by Alicia DeBrincat

Cover design by Kustom Creative

Interior design by Alban Fischer

Author photo by Mark Bennington

CONTENTS

. . . . .

TROGLODYTE

. . . . .

SUPERBABY SAVES SLUGVILLE

• • • • •

By the time my little brother showed up, everyone was pretty much sick and tired of the whole baby thing. The Teamsters were on strike, so our dad was walking picket lines up and down the California coast instead of delivering meat to North Beach and Chinatown butcher shops in his blood-stinky van. Our mom tossed out her hospital slippers, put on black leather pumps, and hopped on a streetcar downtown where her secretarial job was waiting for her to come back to after she popped the little bugger out. She was happier than anything to return to the much-needed overtime and martinis with the "kids," which is what she called anyone her age without children.

Our grandmother had recently gotten divorced. She was finally living the high life, which basically meant her grand-maternal instinct rolled over and stuck all four legs straight up in the air. Instead of enjoying after-school hours in the park with her baby grandson the way she had with me, Grandma spent her afternoons hell-bent on losing the nest egg at Bingo and shopping for dresses that shot off sparks when she did the rumba or the cha-cha. Grandpa made himself scarce in those days, but he showed his red face every now and then to scare the crap out of us, borrow a sawbuck, and then sail away in his beautiful Checker cab number 584, which gleamed like a yellow sunbeam. My youthful, plentiful aunts and uncle were busy wasting time and pocket money on the so-called Summer of Love, so the chore of babysitting my brother fell to me.

We spent our afternoons in Grandma's front yard. Like a jailbird, I separated rocks from dirt clods and dirt from turds in the dried-up cement square, while my brother keened for hours on end in a small wooden box. At first, our antics attracted a slew of visitors. The Hinterlanders, whom our uncle dubbed the Weiners, complained they couldn't hear Merv Griffin over my brother's caterwauls. The Bossanovachiks claimed rearranging the turds confused their dog Maxie (whom our uncle called Muttonhead), which gave her the runs. Bonnie J., who had just recently moved in and didn't know too much about our family, came over to introduce me to her dolly (big whoop). Bonnie J. also brought salt water taffy for me and my brother to share. I immediately announced that his allergy to taffy could be fatal, confiscated his portion, and ate it.

After a few months, my brother's all-out hollering subsided to an incessant whine. The Hinterlanders turned up the TV. The Bossanovachiks switched Maxie's dog food. Cobwebs collected in my brother's ears, and pigeons came to roost on him when the fog broke and the sun came through just right. It was hell cleaning their snow-white shit from his playsuit; the acid devoured the polyester nearly clear through to his skin.

About six months in, my brother got hip to the idea that the standard baby bullshit wasn't going to fly at our house, and that extraordinary measures would be required in order to get any attention. It was on toward winter now, and our pleasant hours in the rock pile had been forcibly relocated indoors. One rainy afternoon, our aunts and I were all home, watching my brother in his cage in the corner of the living room.

The crying and whining had ceased; now all my brother did was sit, wobble from side to side, and chew on the end of a raggedy blanky.

"Do you think he's hungry?" one aunt asked.

"Maybe he's sleepy," suggested another.

"He looks like he's gotta go," said a third.

"I think he's spying on us," said the fourth.

I was watching Merv Griffin and plucking the gold threads from the arm of Grandma's scratchy chesterfield. I said nothing.

Soon our aunts left the room to smoke a cigarette or make a phone call to a boy or girlfriend to complain about my brother's boring behavior. When they returned, my brother was out of his cage, on his back in the middle of the floor.

"What happened?" they asked.

"Merv sang," I said, braiding the gold threads into a wristband.

"No," they said, "your brother."

He was lying on his back, blanky akimbo, glowing in a kind of stunned silence, for once not eating or shitting or sleeping or boring the crap out of us. We picked him up from the floor, returned him to his cage, then went back to ruining our lives and the furniture.

A few minutes later, we all turned around again. Presto! There he was on the floor. No one saw him do it, or heard him land. Naturally, we accused each other of helping him perform this gymnastic escapade. We locked ourselves in the bathroom to prove our innocence, eyeing each other suspiciously in mirrors. When we came out, he was on the floor again, red-faced and radiant. We tossed him back in, and this time we stayed there to watch.

My brother closed his big eyes and curled his tiny fists. With a clairvoyant's calm composure, he scrunched up his face, sucked in a huge breath, then held it until his cheeks were tomatoes. He bellowed an existential moan not unlike the sound our Grandpa made while pushing a conked-out cab up our steep, dead-end street, shivered violently, then levitated and hurled himself over the bars of his cage.

"Wow," one aunt said, nudging his pajama-covered foot with her toe. "He's a Superbaby."

Initially, he was. Superbaby was our shiny new toy, a plaything that delighted our craven appetites for fun. After a few days of amusing the neighbors and scaring their pets, after heated intramural debates over Freak vs. Miracle, Nature vs. Nurture, Roller Derby vs. Football, Raiders vs. 49ers, the best we could figure was Superbaby was ticked off and he wanted some goddamn attention. This emotion gathered in him a kind of metaphysical strength whereby he was able to propel himself short distances. Big whoop. We grew accustomed to Superbaby holding court from the floor. Most of us even learned to step over him. We were effective ignorers. It was in our DNA.

Superbaby's next manipulation transpired in the spring, after a few brave and hearty weeds pushed their green heads through the rock pile. It was one aunt's chore to wash his rotten, stinking diapers every other day, and to add the perfect amount of bleach that would remove stains, eliminate germs, and give Superbaby's sensitive bottom just the right amount of irritation it deserved. Historically, Superbaby was a fantastic crapper. His habits of elimination combined Swiss-clock precision with the visceral nose punch of a Texas cattle ranch. His dirty diaper output kept our aunt's chore on an exacting schedule, one that allowed her greasy boyfriend to hop over the fence every other day so they could make out while she tended the diapers. Like all families in our neighborhood, the washing contraption was kept in a dark shed with cracked and dusty windows, which let in just enough light to encourage the copulations of black widows and teenagers.

But on this particular washday, our aunt was surprised when Superbaby's diaper barrel was empty. No diapers, no load. No load, no washing. No washing, no making out in the shed. After five days of an empty barrel, our aunt was nose-diving toward a hormonal holocaust. It became all too apparent that Superbaby was holding it.

Like dust bunnies under a bed, we were trapped in Superbaby's master plan. We held a meeting and agreed we *had* noticed he was growing. He was now shaped like a septic tank, and our uncle used him as an ottoman to hold his TV dinner while watching the war on the nighttime news. It occurred to us that Superbaby was in danger of exploding. Action was required. We set a date for a house party and called the neighbors in. Obedient slaves we were, puppets on twine, milling around with Cheese Whiz on crackers, oohing and aahing at our monument to perseverance and perversity. Mr. and Mrs. Hinterlander suggested an enema. The Bossanovachiks thought perhaps a plumber. Superbaby lay there beaming like a Buddha, receiving boatloads of attention from his devoted acolytes.

Grandma stood at Superbaby's side with a carton of Rocky Road and announced it was time for dessert. We surrounded her like seagulls, clutching our bowls. Finally, Superbaby was dead center. A drum roll of flatulence sounded, and we responded instantly to its seismic symphony, nostrils a-quiver. A green cloud of noxious vapor gathered over our heads and pelted us with acid rain. We clapped our hands over our faces, but the main event was yet to come. And come Superbaby's supercrap did. A predatory masterpiece, it hissed like a python, threatening to smother us in its deadly embrace. It wound its way around our ankles until we found ourselves chained to the family members or neighbors we despised most. It snatched the Rocky Road from my grandmother's hands, slithered down the front stairs, and disappeared into a crack in the sidewalk, where it seeped into the concrete into a natural spring that was incubating below our home. Once we unchained ourselves from each other, we replaced the ruined carpet, vowed never again to eat Rocky Road, and, most importantly, took turns giving Superbaby enemas if ever he deviated from his scheduled deposits by more than thirty seconds.

It was the first time we'd ever seen him smile.

Finally, summertime. It was freezing cold in San Francisco, with a fierce wind-chill factor. Over the months, the rich, primordial stew of Superbaby's supercrap had mated with our dormant spring, bubbled up from the crack in the sidewalk and created at the bottom of our front stairs the most beautiful river of green slime we had ever seen. We loved it so much we named it. The Pississlippi rendered every foray into the world, and equally every homecoming, a harrowing adventure that threatened life and limb. Better still, thanks to the Pississlippi, what used to be a dry, wizened square of rocks and turds was now a verdant valley, a veritable Nile delta of magical mud that smelled vaguely of shit. Mud that sucked at your feet. Mud that swallowed toys and shoes. Mud that held its shape for building castles and bridges and slabs for virgin sacrifices.

Rampant in all this beautiful mud were extended families of banana slugs. Big mustard granddaddies with foreskin hoods. Shapely mothers with high-pitched, come-hither screams. Horny teenagers with BB guns and cigarettes. Babies no bigger than French fries. Although Superbaby was Slugville's inadvertent creator, under my rule, he became its archenemy. The slugs went to war against their dastardly Gulliver. They crossed oceans of mud to colonize him with their flags. They captured him, cut off his legs, dropped them into their volcano, then melted the rest of him with their flesh-eating slime. It was a marvelous summer.

Until Grandpa started to visit again. At first, he'd show up on Wednesdays, when he knew Grandma would be at the hairdresser's. His uniform reeked of cheap Tenderloin perfume, a motley fragrance of cooking oil, old man underwear, and WD-40. He brought consolation prizes for us all: leftover bags from Cheetah's, his daily diner haunt. The bags usually contained half of something: a cheeseburger, an order of onion rings, the infrequent grilled liver steak with half-strips of real bacon. He'd hand me the bags to disburse among the aunts and uncle, although mostly I just piled them up in the crisper. Then he'd stand at the bottom of the stairs, smoking a cigarette and commenting loudly on the disgraceful condition of the Pississlippi and Slugville. "If I were still living here, I'd concrete this whole mess over," he'd propose. "Then you could play on it real nice." Grandpa always had grandiose beautification plans. At various times before the divorce, he had promised to drive a tractor through the garage to clear out Grandma's newspaper collection (it dated all the way back to the late fifties), to saw off our uncle's bedroom and put it on a raft in the bay, and to install some nice iron bars on the windows of our aunts' rooms to keep out the boys.

This time when Grandpa pulled up, it wasn't a Wednesday at all. It was a Saturday, Grandma's birthday, and there was a party inside the house. The Hinterlanders had donated old *TV Guides* as party favors for everyone. The Bossanovachiks brought puppies. The Bingo team had arrived en masse, and there were even rumors of the return of Rocky Road. Superbaby and I were dressed for the occasion, with Saran Wrap bound around our Sunday shoes while we pounded out the next chapter in Slugville's violent history. In fact, Superbaby might have been over-dressed. He'd had the sniffles the past month or so; now the only way he could play outdoors was in a pale blue, puffed-up snowsuit that made him look like the Michelin Man. His brown eyes bugged out like a frog's under his pale blue snow cap with the ear flaps, pom-poms, and cro-cheted chinstrap. He was one cool Hindenburg of a customer, with the perfect innocent guise to enact his devious escape plan.

I had in my possession four prized and highly-forbidden kitchen matches, which I was going to use to light a possibly defunct sparkler left over from our July Fourth extravaganza in hopes of unleashing a decent volcano on the unwary citizens of Slugville. I was packing dirty kleenex into the volcano's crater for kindling, when a dark shadow crossed the Pississlippi.

With his hands on his hips, and his hat pushed back on his high, pink forehead, Grandpa was like a giant redwood tree, a forest of grandfather, looking down on me and Superbaby, squatting in the outskirts of Slugville. "How's my number-one grandson?" Grandpa picked up Superbaby and twirled him over his head.

Superbaby didn't make a sound. He was sneaky that way.

"How about a jaunt around the block?" Grandpa carried Superbaby under his arm like the Sunday paper and put him in the front seat of his Checker. Number 584 purred like a bright yellow panther; her chrome gleamed under a sudden shaft of sunlight that cracked through the foggy sky. "Fifty bucks and a jaunt around the block with my number-one grandson." Grandpa rubbed his hands together and slammed the car door so hard you could hear the eyes of all the cats and dogs on the block click open from their naps.

Grandpa lit up a Lucky Strike as he strolled back to Slugville. My first match had blown out in a weak whisper of wind. I cupped my hands around the second match, and prayed. This was no regular old flame I desired. I wanted a flame as hot as the dickens, one whose searing heat came straight from holy hell.

"This place is disgusting," Grandpa said. "What you need here is a nice lawn. For five bucks, I could roll out some sod and put up a nice swing set."

A lawn? A swing set? What did he think we were, a bunch of babies? "That's what parks are for," I muttered, trying not to sound ungrateful without losing my place in my prayer. If we lost Slugville, we lost everything.

It didn't matter; he wasn't listening. "How about you, Eileen?" Grandpa hollered up at the house. "You wanna go for a jaunt with me and the boy?" He twirled his cap on the index finger of his free hand.

Everyone upstairs was peeking out from behind the curtains, sucking on spoons of Rocky Road to separate the marshmallows and walnuts from the ice cream. No one noticed Superbaby sitting in the cab, or that number 584's motor was running.

Grandpa inhaled his cigarette all the way down to the filter, then flicked it into Slugville's tributary, where it plopped and sizzled menacingly. He forded the Pississlippi in his black leather boots, leaving wet, green prints as he climbed the stairs up to the front door. Grandpa knocked the knocker till one of our aunts cracked the door, while I quickly hid the soggy butt in my coat pocket.

There was an abomination of curses as Grandpa pushed his way indoors, and the yelling started almost instantly. Even as I was focusing on striking the match and catching its small, bug-sized flame to a soggy corner of kleenex, I knew that our dad and Mr. Hinterlander and Mr. Bossanovachik and probably even our uncle and the Bingo team, too, had surrounded Grandpa and pushed him back out the door, which got shut again so hard you could hear the little peephole door on the inside clang open and closed from the force. "All I need is fifty bucks," Grandpa bellowed, his lips at the peephole. "Fifty lousy bucks!"

Grandpa's face was red when he turned toward the street. He clomped down the stairs, making sure each footstep was loud and scary and made the wood slats creak. He stopped at the bottom stair and began to whistle, clear and loud and pitch-perfect. "Good night, Eileen. Eileen, good night." He lit a fresh cigarette, re-positioned his hat just so on his head. "I'll be damned!" he said, before lunging back up the stairs with his tree-long legs, whistling all the while. The old fart was going back in. Sure, they said no to fifty; maybe they'd be good for twenty-five just to get him to leave. It had worked before.

As Grandpa was working up to another knock, back in number 584, Superbaby's plan was falling into place. Superbaby tried to stand up at the window to wave bye-bye, cute little sap that he was, but the puffed-up snowsuit monkeyed with his balance. His eyes got bigger as he fell backwards away from the window and onto the taxi's long bench front seat. I could hear his muffled laughter over the engine's lopsided rumble. Superbaby climbed back to his feet, grabbing onto the steering wheel for leverage, then continued to pull himself up by grabbing the gearstick that poked out from behind. The clunk was decisive as the engine's rumble straightened out and the car shifted into reverse.

Grandpa turned from the front door toward the street just as the taxi began to inch backwards. Superbaby was waving wildly in the window as the taxi rolled down the hill away from our house.

"Who's driving that car?" Grandpa cried out, but of course, I ignored him.

If my brother wanted to leave, I thought he jolly well should. It was no surprise to me that he would want to get the hell out. I struck another match and this one caught. I was able to light both the tissue and the sparkler, and I screamed as silver sparks shot out of Slugville's volcano and tiny plumes of grey smoke rose from the pink kleenex lava. Now it was time for a rainstorm. I dumped a jar of murky, brown water into the volcano's crater. The water cut a trail through Slugville's main road, taking a couple of houses with it, as well as the fire station that had already been demolished by an earthquake caused by the spaceship landing and subsequent pillaging by the evil serial killers. The carnage was comprehensive and satisfying.

Grandpa stepped his size-fourteen boot into the middle of Slugville's main square and grabbed my arm. "I said who took your goddamned brother, and you better answer me before I take this goddamn pile of mud and dump it into the bay." He yelled it with the kind of growl that usually only came out when he was about to whale on our uncle.

"Nobody," I yelled back. "He's escaping all by himself." I pointed down the hill, past the Hinterlanders' with the gingerbread trim that made you think a giant cuckoo was going to pop out of the front door. "And goddamn it, you're messing up Slugville!"

Grandpa turned white, as though a shade pulled down over his face. He took off running, and it was kind of funny how his expression changed when his muddy boots hit the Pississlippi and lost all traction. His tree legs flew up and his whole body became an airborne V, which was how we drew birds in art class sometimes when we were in a hurry to get to the good stuff like the wars and the battlefields and the nurses and the sex. He hit the ground hard on his bottom and out came a word I'd only seen written on a bathroom wall till then. More importantly, Slugville was safe from disaster.

Meanwhile, the taxi's big chrome grill was shrinking; it was already past the Bossanovachiks' with the gated front yard where Maxie furiously guarded the house and her puppies, and now its back end was veering toward the middle of the street.

At the bottom of the hill, Mrs. J.'s green station wagon turned the corner and was starting to climb. Probably bringing Bonnie J. home from ballet lessons so they could come to Grandma's party. Bonnie J. with the tutu who never wanted to play in Slugville. The last time she came over, she just gave her dolly the bottle to make her wet her diaper. Bonnie J. changed that dolly's underwear so much, I offered to toss it into our volcano to teach it a lesson. I could see Bonnie J.'s queer-shaped head in the backseat, like a tiny Mr. Peanut. Now Mrs. J. was blowing the horn. Number 584 with Superbaby inside had picked up alarming speed and was headed straight for Mrs. J. and Bonnie.

This looked promising. I stuffed the last match in my pocket and ran yelling past Grandpa, who sat paralyzed in the Pississlippi, scratching his head. I was halfway to catching up when Mrs. J. laid on the horn. Her eyeballs were wide as she hand-over-handed the giant steering wheel. The station wagon careened away from me, jumped the curb and smacked into the fire hydrant in front of Mrs. J.'s own house.

A geyser of brown water, which could only have come from our underground lake, shot into the air and arced across the Hinterlanders' front yard. Hundreds of millions of rainbows hung in the polluted mist.

Bonnie J. leaped out of the backseat and ran over to me. I grabbed her hands and we began jumping and screaming, jumping and screaming, jumping and screaming, jumping and screaming, jumping and screaming. It was the best thing that ever happened on our block, and it was all thanks to Superbaby, who had continued down the hill in number 584, and was already out of sight.

GLOSSOLALIA

·····

Gazelle legs splay out, neck muscles ripple fine she dainty swig dark emerald murk at summer water hole.

Empty belly alligator imitate vicious, hungry log, blink watchful amber eye.

Shady banyan branch. Hippo bead on both, sigh over tasty business mossy bottom lettuce.

Without half try, alligator lazy snap ragged jaws.

Gazelle, mid-swallow, caught in vise of yellow, pointy teeth.

Alligator think, "Ha! Lunch!" Saliva drool for gazelle bonbon of loin & ankle, ear & thigh.

Hippo, she say, "Fuck that shit!" Make Nijinsky leap into blood-streak whirlpool, knock alligator on the bean, pluck gazelle from slack-jaw astonish, & lay her gentle on riverbank, out of daze old lizard reach.

Alligator slink down fast. Eye blast venom, appetite.

Hippo nudge gazelle sable head into her mouth, cushion fat pink tongue under skull like a pillow.

"Ha! Lunch redux!" alligator spit.

But no.

Hippo whisper secrets into blissful, ignorant gazelle. Say, "Moon is cotton

& she laugh all night. Birds sing to measure the age of the world. Fish rather dance than swim. Time to run. Time to run."

Gazelle open eyes, crusty & surprise. Wishbone lungs fill with river-horse secrets, heart pound like prayer as she birth herself from hippo mouth, bow once, & scamper Bambi-style, dribbling urine like to say, "Man! Did you catch that?"

Mommy reach over shut the TV from her folding chair. "Dora, what you got to say?"

"Them Hollywood animals," I say from bed, "went to acting school. Gonna get treats and a paycheck." Just 'cause I sick don't mean I shut up. Don't mean I can't think.

"Ain't no tricks on the 'National Geographical'." Mommy smile because she say it wrong on purpose. She look down her lap. "Porter, what about you?"

Porter, he a big boy. Already 10, but Mommy lap he favorite seat. Still consider nature like a bible. Think a long time before respond. "Everybody know hippo vegemarian," Porter finally say, snuggle down to Mommy like he want back inside. "Wasn't never gonna eat no gazelle."

"Even more." Mommy ease Porter from between her bones. "Hippo give that little skinny the fresh minty breath of life."

Lyle Beauty come stand the doorway, rub he hands up under he shirt, show stripe hair down he belly. "You and them kids finish that TV? How you feel, Dora?" He pretend care, but everyone know "Wrestlemania" start 2 minutes. He a big child like that. Just want what he want.

"Take it," Mommy say. She flinch when Lyle Beauty yank the plug & haul the TV out the room. Her eye track down he behind way our pumpkin cat Violet sometime stare off in a corner like she waiting on a message from the wall. In looks department, Mommy definitely gazelle, especially when her eyes on fire for Lyle Beauty.

Porter put he hand on Mommy face, move it back he direction. "God tell hippo do that?" Porter ask, think maybe God is cool.

"Maybe he didn't and maybe he did. What matter hippo did it," Mommy say. "Dora, put this boy to bed." She place her mouth on he head like a pretend kiss, not the real kind with the noise so you know you been kiss, then run out the room. "And don't forget wash his hands first."

Porter hands much littler than mine & way he look so happy when I wash them make me want to squeeze them real hard, make him cry out. But not tonight. He so full of questions about the hippo, I got to pinch him make him stop. Tuck him in tight like envelope, then go back to bed, listen Mommy & Lyle Beauty laugh they secrets while "Wrestlemania" audience cheer.

Today I get restrict to home quarantine. Grammy come over from number 9 before Mommy leave for work at Chateau de Style, where she specialize hair design. "Ain't you gone wear that mask like doctor said?" Mommy ask Grammy, dragging Porter behind her. He still mad at me for not letting him dress like a pirate for school. Pretend to be slow & sleepy zombie boy, suck he thumb & don't open he eyes he ain't got to.

"Why I need a mask for? That girl just got plain 'fluenza," Grammy say. She got her pee-yellow canary Mitch with her, fussing with seeds & making sure old Violet lock in the bathroom before she put Mitchie cage on the table.

Different kind of quiet begin Mommy shut the door. Quiet, until you listen hard. But Grammy teakettle hum. Mitch cheep like a baby chick. Violet howl & scratch the door. Bus brakes hiss a nightmare snake, maybe anaconda. Quiet like a jungle circus.

Only thing on TV "Hogan's Heroes." Already I bore this sickly life. Slip between the velvet drape & dirty window, I secret spy on the courtyard our own Pyracantha Lysander Arms, where Lyle Beauty stand in shade behind the fluffy-prickly tree. He watch a new tenant move in. He call it supervise. Her name Miss Juniper. Lyle Beauty he know insides all Grammy 15 apartments like his own stanky underwear. Know Mr. & Miz Vazquez, number 3, got 2 sets bunk beds in that tiny 2-bedder. Know McDermotts, number 5, everything they bring shroud in blue plastic tarp & "Hog-tie like dead bodies," Lyle Beauty say at dinner. Always make me wonder how them pigs put on they ties.

Lyle Beauty tap the key ring he knee & smile. 15 keys make hefty clank.

"What you watching, Dora?" Grammy flip a finger through the curtains & we secret agent them both. Reporting for duty, Colonel Hogan.

Miss Juniper she don't bring much except hammock & a harp. Sad eyes & bag groceries. Bottles clinking. Lyle Beauty, he wait she drag that harp upstairs, then go help put them groceries up. She give him a bottle & they talk soft 'bout hammock-style sleep. He even take extra 10 help her nail both ends, not to mention the eyeshot of pure natural breast inside the lawn-green fabric her blouse. Oh, she know it. Swing & laugh. Promise let Lyle Beauty run his callous hands her golden harp.

When Grammy rap the window, Lyle Beauty see us. He finger twitch without him mean to, like electric shock.

I know he want smoke. He ain't smoke since Mommy catch him sniff that last babysitter Nicholette. No one know, but I secret agent that, too. Lyle Beauty make me swear keep it secret or Mommy tan he hide & mine. I never say nothing, but I know Lyle scamming get some more Miss Juniper. He have ways, he think. I practically see thinky words float up over his head, all crinkly & black, fresh-type against light-brown sky.

Lyle Beauty, he just tap them keys against he thigh. I hope they leave a bruise.

Crying baby sound make me & Grammy jump. "Go let that nasty feline creature out the bathroom," Grammy say. "Mitchie back his cage."

After lunch, me & Grammy glue macaroni to Styrofoam for Xmas ornaments. Miz Vazquez bring over XXL cardboard box. "Got a new refrigerator," she say. "Thought Dora, being sick, might like to play inside."

"New refrigerator," Grammy say. "Must be nice."

"Not really," Miz Vazquez say. "I got to have my appendix remove. My sister sent some money help with the hospital bill. Dagobert, he think we gone have just enough left over." Miz Vazquez smile my way. "You let me know you got anything you want me keep cold."

"Roger Wilco," I say. I spy with my little eye, she got scare behind her mind.

"I like to freeze old Lyle Beauty hammer," Grammy say, then she whisper something Miz Vazquez & they howl almost to tears.

Lyle Beauty make box a clubhouse in the living room, slice a window with he knife. He laugh 'cause it say THIS END UP on the side the box, with a arrow point at my little face inside.

When Porter get home, he want in the club. Knock he door, make the whole house shake.

"Can't you read?" I point where I wrote PRIVATE above the door.

"No," Porter say.

"Verboten!" I say, like Colonel Klink. "You can't come in without the code."

"Cat puke?" Porter guess, because Violet do that right now on the carpet.

"Nuh," I say. "I was thinking 'spats.'"

"Oh, yeah, 'spats' good," he say. Porter got them brown eyes people always know what he think. Clubhouse look real fine to him. Nice safe place be inside.

"Guess again." I want him be good & jealous my clubhouse, like I'd be if he was the one sick instead me.

"Suspenders?"

I stick my tongue out. "Fur ball." Porter can't imagine I could change it every time, but I can.

"Why your tongue brown?" he ask.

Grammy tell him, "Take your behind outdoors, Mister Porter."

I stuck indoor clubhouse rest the day, until Mommy home Chateau de Style. "That box stink like hog heaven, Dora. It got to go outside."

Lyle Beauty take it out the courtyard. I wonder do they wear ties in hog heaven.

Still quarantine & too tired play. Think maybe I got the plague or something, feel so woozy always. Now everyone got to wear the paper mask, everyone mouth & nose wiggle up & down they talk. Look like they got a hand stuck up they throat, like sock puppets.

Grammy make me write thanky note for when Miz Vazquez get out the hospital. It say: *Dear Miz V. I hope they let you bring home your appendix. I would like to see it. Thank you for the box. It a perfect clubhouse & Porter can't come in. I hope you get well soon & me too. Dora, number 2.*

Spoil in my glory, Grammy let me lick frosting off eggbeaters & test chicken skin, check burnt crispy like everyone like. She cool washcloth my forehead & open up my hand, read my lines. "You're going to live a long and colorful life," she say, trace finger to wrist, make me squirm. It tickle good till I cough like barking dog & Grammy have to whack my back make me stop.

I secret agent Porter play outside. He know I kill him he go inside my clubhouse, so he sit next to it, like sitting near just as good. He make his hands like a bowl & stare into them, talking words nonstop. Maybe he read he own lines like Grammy do mine.

When I bore of secret agent Porter, I help Grammy clean the canary cage. "So much fun," Grammy say. "Look how happy it make Mitchie when his paper clean."

"Sure," I say, like I so sick I don't know difference between fun & birdshit. Maybe that's a result my colorful life.

"Remember," Grammy say, "funnies side up."

That's when I hear Porter laugh outside. All by himself, little weirdo, knocking knees together & falling over onto scraggle grass. He stare in his old hand bowl like it some kind of crystal ball, nod his head like he promise do whatever it say

"Porter psycho," I say. "Look." Grammy join me at the window. We all use watching Porter do he things. One: He keep a bag of rocks under he pillow. Two: Every rock got a name. Three: He say he abduct by aliens. This happen mostly on Wednesdays.

Mitchie get crazy being out the cage. Try to fly at Grammy's shoulder but misfire & bump my head, which scare the crap out him. "Mitchie just did it on my shoulder," I say. More colorful by the minute.

"Porter splendid boy and Mitchie splendid bird," Grammy croon, all squeaky-bird voice. Cup Mitchie in her hands, press Avon Lady lips to beak, & padlock him safe back in he cage.

"They might be splendid and all, but I still feel like socking both them," I tell her.

"Go wash your face, nasty girl." She pinch my arm so I know she mean it.

When I go the bathroom, Violet spit up another pile in the corner. Puke look like a little mouse, sound asleep on cold pink tile. I fetch a towel to clean it & a small book fall out the shelf.

Dear diary, Mommy write. I skip through the boring part, where Mommy dream she might like to write some day. Fixing hair nice & all & she got the knack for find people pretty side, yes, she do. But she like to tell the kind story all Mommy gonna tell every Baby & Baby gonna remember all they life. The kind story start with love & hate & end with something new. Mommy wish for drugs. Not the old kind, made her fly & wild. She want the heal kind—kind free her mind & open her soul. Kind that fillet people heart, let in the ones need forgive, the Hitlers & the Mansons. The Papa Royales. The Lyle Beauty.

I get all romantic behind my eyes. Page back where Mommy first meet Lyle Beauty. Mommy write: *When that beautiful mouth says cigar, I know he means he wants me to rest my head between his legs and give him one fine blow job. He says it like this: see-gar. He's got a way with my sweet spot that keeps me thinking of him all day long, making it hard to concentrate from payday to payday, between cutting heads and playing Solitaire. "Casaba," he said once, pulling me out into the courtyard in the dead of night, behind the hibiscus tree, right under Mrs. Vazquez' window. I will never forget his tongue, bitter brown from coffee, his hands pulling my sweater from my skirt, the steam, Spanish radio and cutlery clattering above us.*

I remember first time I meet Lyle Beauty. Birthday party, Porter 6 year old. Lyle Beauty, he move in Pyracantha Lysander Arms number 7 that day. Porter circle he new trike in the courtyard.

Lyle Beauty stand center, like hole in a sugar donut. Chocolate pants, Pendleton shirt, hands in pockets, gold tooth whistle "Yankee Doodle." Hot spots from Grammy handheld flash glare on Lyle Beauty shiny cheeks. Already act like Papa Royale even though everybody know Porter real Papa Royale made like a banana & split.

Mommy watch Lyle Beauty watch Porter so hard her cake knife frosting drop to dirt. Hippo watching alligator watch gazelle.

He said he loved me so much he wanted to break all the bones in my arms and legs. He wanted to reset them in the shape of a perfect instrument. He wanted to spray-paint me gold, stretch catgut from my shin to my shoulder, play music on me like a symphony between love and heaven. His words made me smudged and blurry, as though I was trying to breathe something solid (earth?) through something light (feathers?). I held my breath, in case it was my last. Lord help me, I cannot resist that man.

I wonder what's blow job & promise myself: Never fall for love or man with Beauty in his name.

Wednesday morning, Mommy dress up for Chateau de Style client Felix. "Look like you doing more than Felix hair," Lyle Beauty say, all thick & spicy mean.

"How many times I gotta say Felix play the other team," Mommy snap.

After breakfast, I secret agent Lyle Beauty sniff around Miss Juniper door, fingering he hammer. He just about to swing her hammock when Porter scream from the courtyard. Everyone live in the

Pyracantha Lysander Arms know that shrieky scream. It mean the aliens come again.

Lyle Beauty, he run away Miss Juniper door, go pick up Porter, pat his back. A cough come up real bad on me till Grammy give me air from the scuba diver tank.

Afternoon Mommy come home sad. Say Felix sister just die from blood-sick disease don't nobody can even say, barely the doctors. Felix say he sister weakly anyhow & ain't never been the same since they baby brother die. He write a eulogy & want Mommy read it since she dream of being a writer, but Mommy say no: If Felix make her cry while she cutting hair, she might chop off his ear & then they both feel bad.

"I feel bad," Porter say, but smiling like he don't know what he say.

"Why?" Mommy put down her fork.

"Aliens came today." Lining up rocks around he dinner plate, which give Grammy the crazy eyes.

"What them aliens say?"

Porter take a big swallow air, don't look at no one when he talk. "They come to kill me because I mad at Dora she sick all the time and boss the clubhouse. I wish God could kill Dora, so aliens say they gonna kill me."

Mommy say, "Not true. Can't be killing no one with wishes."

"If you could kill people with wishes, Porter be dead about thousand times," I holler. My head hurts & I want to play outside. I want to take off my clothes & roll in dirt, even though it night, & getting dirty don't make no sense. I want to kill stupid Mitchie. My tongue hurt.

Mommy open her mouth, then she close it & just look sad.

Lyle Beauty look at me like he wish he could kill me, like he wish God would strike me dead or alligator come & eat me up, take awful girl away from everybody happy splashy pond. He turn to Porter. "God just make certain people mean, Porter. It ain't your fault. That girl knows where she's going when she die."

I hate everything. Everyone. My wishbone lungs tight from wishing I die. They be wailing about miss me every minute & what a fine child I was & smart. I'ma fly around with angels on my shoulders. I don't never need to walk, just ride the teacups instead or catch a car down the Matterhorn I want get somewhere real fast. And all the animals my best friends, even the alligator, who would chew Lyle Beauty in half with one good yellow-tooth chomp I wiggle my littlest finger.

Next night, Mr. Vazquez come over, ask can the triplets stay for supper, he got to make some arrangements. He say when the doctors dig in Lola appendix, they find cancer. They try scoop it all out, but too late. Lola she just expire. He so creep out, he can't even go the kitchen no more without see the refrigerator & think of Lola.

I never know Miz Vazquez first name Lola. Sound so close to Dora. I crumple up the thanky note my PJ pocket.

Grammy make special fry chicken just because triplets company. Triplets don't say nothing. No one know which one which anyhow. They let me finish all they crispy chicken skin & flash! A sword fly through my stomach. I take a giant pill and lay down straight to bed.

Matter of fact, my funeral ain't like Disneyland at all. Ain't no stuffed animals, no teacups. I look just like myself in the pine box against the pink satin. My black hair's real shiny & curled like a princess, even though the lady part the bangs on the wrong side, so when I look down at me, I look just like I use to look, only backwards, like in a mirror. & then I wonder am I backwards in the mirror or myself in the mirror & backwards in real life? I got lots time to think on that kind of stuff, philosophy & things I always curioused about but never got to really ponder deep because Violet always puking or Porter doing his strangeness or needing hands washed.

It just like every other day in the Pyracantha Lysander Arms, except I ain't around. First day, the fever sweep in & take me, nobody talk a whole day. After my funeral, everyone sit in the living room round the TV, except the TV not on, & everyone still looking at it, like a habit in they necks they just can't break. Porter, he been a pirate all day long. He go play my clubhouse with his bag of rocks & nobody say jack-crap.

Mommy clear her throat & blow her nose. "My piece chicken had blood in it." She say this straight to the TV, but Grammy know who she really talking at.

"Don't you blame my cooking. Dora had fine, long lines in her hands. You got to blame anyone, go blame God." She squeak back & forth in old rocking chair, holding Mitchie her hands like she praying on him & blowing kissy at he beak.

"Dora sure would be fine she got a chance to grow up," Lyle Beauty say quiet, shaking change in the pocket his dress pants & looking out the window, where Miss Juniper in the courtyard, smoking a cigarette & sucking on a beer bottle, sitting next to the clubhouse Porter inside.

"Don't talk like that about my baby girl," Mommy say, sharp & scissors.

Lyle Beauty swing he head around, show Mommy he surprise face. Sun in he eye make it toffee caramel, like my favorite apples. Lots words floating between them, swirling around like planets & stars, none them said out loud.

"Sometimes it don't matter who you love or how much, they die." Grammy act like she talking to Mitchie, but everybody listen anyhow. "Lotta people say people die in threes. Losing Dora one them things. Just bad luck."

Mommy stand up. Her whole body shaking like gazelle when it come out the hippo mouth. "Now Dora dead, there's no need for quarantine," Mommy tell Grammy. "I'm going to the bathroom. You be gone by the time I get back."

Grammy make her mouth like a line. Grab Mitchie in he birdcage with he shitty funny papers & head on home across the courtyard, number 9. Her door slam so loud, Lyle Beauty jump & got to pretend he meant to shake that pocket change.

"I'm gone outside for a smoke," he say, only no one left to hear it.

Mommy pull her diary from behind stack of towels. She write: *Every morning for the rest of my life, when I wake, I'll look in my coffee cup and see a bloody head emerging from my ripped vagina. I will never stop thinking about Dora. I will never stop hating God. If I were to write a story now, it would be about a soldier and a nurse during wartime. Severed limbs hang from cypress trees like fleshy beans. I know how it feels to breathe dirt, to eat it. To nourish my belly with hate. I'll describe long lines of scarecrow me, in bandages and uniforms, shooting their best friends for a slice of moldy bread.* Mommy arm tire from all the hate come out of it, but she got more to write.

"Let Jesus carry you," Miss Juniper saying Porter. "He take care a you now your sister gone."

"You mean like aliens carry me?" Porter ask, he bare foot petting on Violet. Violet yawn & stretch, keep one eye on her boy.

"Ain't no such thing aliens." Miss Juniper suddenly Queen of All Knowledge.

"Yuh huh." Porter expert, don't care what no amateur think.

"Where they come from then?" Miss Juniper ask.

"Everyone know the sky," Porter answer. Can't believe Miss Juniper don't know that. Even Dora know that, he think. Knew.

I want tell him, duh, even babies know that, but not sure how he hear me.

"What they do when you see them?" Miss Juniper talking sexy, like Porter grown man.

"Aliens say I'm bad and deserve die," Porter explain. Pay more attention he rocks, making designs in circles & squares.

"Nobody deserve to die." Miss Juniper touch Porter shoulder. "Seven lambs say God want us all go heaven."

"Hog heaven," I yell 'cause it feel good & I think it will make Porter laugh, but he don't hear I guess. He squirm away Miss Juniper arm like Violet do when you pet long down her back & she slink down caterpillar-ish, only Porter more polite. Good for him. That one got too much Jesus in her eye. Don't mean she shut up.

Now Lyle Beauty step outside the shadow the tree he been smoking under. "Porter hard to understand sometime. Stuff he say sound like he talk in tongues."

Miss Juniper look up at him like he the sun, & she bask he golden glow. "That's all right, Mr. Beauty," she say. "Perhaps he blessed. Everybody got to have something fall back on."

Lyle Beauty say, "You mean like my good looks?"

Miss Juniper smile. "That's one thing." Now she finish her bottle, she talk better, like she younger than she used to be. "Could be talent. Skill. Prayer if you like."

"How about I just say the alphabet backwards?" Lyle Beauty ask. "Or talk in code?"

"Password 'spats,'" Porter say, but nobody notice. Them two only got eyes for theyselves.

Mommy come outside now, shake her write arm like it tired & empty, shade her eye try decipher whatever going on the clubhouse. "What everybody doing?"

"Miss Juniper just say she play us some harp," Lyle Beauty say.

"Oh, no," Miss Juniper mouth say, but her eyes say, "Hell, yeah, and you better watch me."

"I don't think so," Mommy say. Her eyes match her mouth.

Miss Juniper muscle her harp down the stairs, hug her thighs round that old-school instrument. After her angel song, Lyle Beauty say, "Your hands so beautiful. I want to pound them paper-thin, bake them into pies and put them on a windowsill."

Miss Juniper so sad & thirsty, wrap in her magic music shawl, see some kind of future instead the crazy behind Lyle Beauty eye.

"Huh," Mommy huff like bull, her high-heel sandal paw the ground like to kick Miss Juniper lights out or whack Lyle Beauty on the lips. She pick up Porter, remind everybody who the rooster in who henhouse.

Miss Juniper don't know stop from go. She pat Porter on he head. "What about them aliens? They do anything nasty to you?" She brave now everybody know she high on Lyle Beauty list. "Make you take off your pants?" Miss Juniper whisper. "I hear you get abduct by real aliens, they leave a mark on your ass. You got proof?"

Porter, he no fool. "Fuck that shit," he say. That make me smile. I remember the day I teach him that one.

Miss Juniper sigh & look to thoughts of tongue-talk calm her down. "Proof of aliens a sign on your ass. Look, I'll show you mine." She flip up the back her plaid skirt & hike up the elastic of her pants, where a large bruise luminate. It all purple, green, & yellow, almost big as Porter's hand when he place it on her thigh.

Lyle Beauty sock him. "Don't touch, Porter."

Porter open he mouth to cry, but he don't make no sound. Just thick string snot stroll down his lip.

Mommy slap Lyle Beauty, who flash pull back he fist high at Mommy. "Verboten!" I say. "Like hell you will. Step back, Jack. Don't cry, McFly."

Porter eyes go wide & he look around. "Dora?" Wind pass through the fluffy-prickly tree like river rush on rocks. Blow through Miss Juniper harp like Sunday harmonica. Blow through Lyle Beauty man parts like ocean wave. Blow through Mommy heart like baby laughter. Everything heavy & slow.

Porter look up at Mommy with old-man knowledge eyes. "Sound like Dora happy voice," he say. "Like when Dora use sing her TV songs."

Mommy smile. She know I love themes. "What Dora happy voice say?"

"Say don't hate God. Ain't God fault she dead. She told me forgive God like you got to forgive the alligator need his lunch."

Mommy give Porter kiss, take him inside.

Lyle Beauty come home late that night. Mommy know what in his eye clear across the room. Before they start throwing yell words, Violet hunch in front the TV & yack up something awful black & hairy.

"Violet kill something," Porter say, inspecting real close. "Plus grass."

Lyle Beauty sit down hard under Mommy glare. "It tournament night," he say. "Someone else got to clean that up."

"That's it," Mommy say. "I can't take any more suffering. Violet got to go. Mean thing probably carry fever that kill my darling Dora."

I never been call darling before. It feel nice.

Mommy wrap Mrs. Violet Deathbed in Porter old blanket. Take Mrs. V. D. to the vet emergency & say, "Go ahead. Put her down."

But the vet put on he metal vest like Lancelot. Sniff Mrs. Violet Deathbed up & down, poke her to & fro. He say, "Not this cat, lady. Not today."

Mommy take Violet home & yell at Lyle Beauty, "Why I lose my baby Dora and get stuck with this bitch?"

Next morning, Mommy won't get up.

"What I suppose do," Lyle Beauty holler. Then he disappear.

Mommy jump up from the bed to secret agent Lyle Beauty behind the velvet curtain. Watch him go Miss Juniper. Talk low & her door closing soft.

Mommy say, "Fine." Real hard. Like spit come out when she say it. "Fine."

Porter, he stay home, too. Dress like a pirate & chef up all the meals for him & Mommy all day long. She call him Captain Cook & Porter don't see no aliens all day.

Mommy washing every dish because that's how many Porter use. From the whole week. Nice & slow. Hot water steam the windows. Spider in the corner web spin crazy around her carcass. "Grammy probably in her chair right now, waiting for me to call," Mommy tell Porter. "Old bitch wait for me to call even when Grammy got time to call, and she know I don't because when she finally does, she say, 'It's been ten days since you call,' and I'll say, 'Already? I just call you,' and she say, 'Yes, that's how it would feel to you wouldn't it? You always too busy to call,' and I say, 'So you calling now, let's talk,' and Grammy say, 'You know what I mean,' and I say, 'So do you.'"

Porter laugh at Mommy speech.

Mommy almost smile. "Whoever invented rubber gloves, I like to marry them," she say.

Porter pour milk over Frosted Flakes & put it on the floor for Violet.

Down in number 15, jazz play so soft you can barely hear Billie, but still Miss Juniper & Lyle Beauty swinging. "What's your front name?" he ask, move he kiwi fruits across her cupcakes.

"Blousie," she giggle, wave her pineapple he banana.

"I truly admire the way your head attach your neck," Lyle Beauty say, making sure the candle light up he teeth when he say it, make he words sparkle. "I want to peel back your skin with a paring knife, reveal your fine-sculpt muscle and gorgeous, blood-fill vertebrae. Excuse me. I'll be right back." Lyle belly-crawl away, run water in the kitchen. Call Mommy, number 2.

"I bet that Grammy," Mommy tell Porter when the phone ring.

"I love you so much," Lyle Beauty whisper Miss Blousie Juniper avocado princess phone. "Your gold and your strings and your symphony."

Mommy listen background noise: radio scratch & Blousie snatch. Mommy hang up & stand quiet think. Feel like a long time before actual words appear. Actual idea. She call Grammy say good-bye, tell Porter put on his pirate suit & pack he rocks. Give Miss Blousie Juniper the fucking cat.

Mommy take Porter Greyhound. She buy ticket number 57 & leave the driving to them. Porter spread he rocks on the next seat over, line up angel light vs. devil blaze. Mommy want to remind him: she hippo, Porter gazelle, but Mommy think Porter already know. He smart that way. Mommy open her diary. So many blanks, so many lines and spaces she want to fill.

Greyhound finally stop far out the city. Way out. Galaxies away. Air hot & dry, buildings low & old. Porter surprise. "You never told me sky so big," he say.

Mommy say, "I never knew."

Mommy & Porter walk the road. Find Sunshine Café, where a bell go off when Mommy open the door. Sunshine clouds & nature all paint up on the walls. Five empty tables & a doorway hung with strings of beads. "They diamonds?" Porter ask.

"Could be," Mommy say.

Person come out from the beads. Mommy can't say it man or woman. Got hair lady-long on one side, gentleman short the other. Face like a gate or a horse, but Mommy squint her eye to find the pretty side. Few snips here & there.

Mommy order cup of tea, peanut butter sandwich for Porter. Tea come with leaves & flowers tie up in a fancy bag. Mommy hate to wet it, but he/she/it say, "Girl, you got to live some time."

Mommy take her tea, sit in somebody old red chair out the garden. Porter watch a green & blue stripe honeybee dig holes in about 100 different places & never stop.

Mommy watch Porter watch a bee.

XMAS OF LOVE

. . . . .

Nothing really happens until the eggs come. Every year it's the same. Trina stands on the closed toilet lid and imagines them behind closed eyes: the Santa platter with the special little ponds to hold them upright, the sunshine white and yellow boats, the light rain of paprika.

Grandma Bunny dips her fingers in a jar of aquamarine goo and pulls Trina's crown into a bathing cap vise, snapping the rubber band from the morning paper around the shortest pinch of a brown tail and anchoring it with a green velveteen bow, lodging the clip deep into Trina's scalp.

"Not so tight, mama." Maureen watches, balancing on the side of the claw foot tub, tapping cigarette ashes into the sink.

"I have to pull them tight and use lots of goo. Girl's hair's like Astroturf." Grandma Bunny slathers more blue gel into Trina's hair.

It drips into Trina's skull, thick and cold and creepy. She shivers, delighted.

"Okay, Tree, look." Grandma Bunny wipes gooey hands on her apron.

"I can't. My eyes won't open. My hair's too tight."

"If you can fly around the room on angel's wings, you can open your eyes. Now, open your damn eyes." Grandma Bunny flicks the back of Trina's head with a sharp index finger.

The murky pink bathroom comes into focus. Trina looks into the cracked mirror above the sink, where she can see herself all the way down to her black Mary Janes.

"Like it?" Grandma catches Trina around the waist with a dishrag.

Trina hops in front of the mirror, imagining brown ringlets bouncing. "It's good," she says, noticing the small pores of Maureen's clear skin, the thickening waist beneath her velvet granny gown. "Your stomach is like an egg," Trina teases, poking Maureen's belly. "Eggs that don't go to the store grow up to be baby chicks," she announces, proud of her knowledge of sex and the world. "Will you hatch a giant baby chick?"

Maureen rolls her eyes and drags dramatically on the cigarette.

Grandma Bunny laughs. "Now *that* would be a miracle."

"Are the eggs ready?" Trina shimmies with anticipation, hoppity, nonstop jumps.

Grandma swats Trina's butt. "Go wait by the tree now. Scoot."

Trina takes inventory of the living room while she waits for Christmas Eve to officially begin: the triangular tree on the mantel made from empty cat food cans wrapped in thick ribbons and decorated with bells; angels of macaroni and Styrofoam, sprayed thick and runny gold; felt scrap mistletoe; a newspaper Santa; her two presents.

Mary enters with a long slim red cigarette poised between tapered lacquered fingers. Fashion-wise, she's in her Chinese phase—red polyester tunic with a dragon on the back, black polyester pajama pants and little flat ballet slippers—and has just prepared her official offering for the Christmas buffet. "I opened a can of black olives," she says, expiring onto the scratchy, brown mohair couch. "With holes, the kind you like."

"No, thanks," Trina says. Finger-hole olives are okay on regular days, but only deviled eggs count at Christmas. "Where's my mom and dad?"

"They went with Auntie Margaret to get John from the hospital."

"Does that mean he'll poop now?" Trina wonders about this every morning, making great snakes that don't break, snakes of beautiful stink and rich color. "He keeps it in his stomach for days sometimes. Why does he do that?"

"We're not sure, honey." Mary arranges herself in the center of the couch, smoothing out her tunic, crossing her ankles just right. "That's why we worry about him. That's why he cries. But nobody worries about you. You're just fine. You're perfect."

Trina and Mary stand in front of the Nativity scene arranged atop the television set. The manger is empty. Trina's favorite cow, like Elsa from the milk carton, lies peaceful and serene on her knees in packing-crate hay. Mary dangles her wrist in front of Trina's face. A jangly, sparkly bracelet. "Red gave me this for Christmas last year. He gave me lots of things." Red hasn't been around for some time, but no one ever mentions that.

Trina runs a finger across the pointy bright rhinestones. "All I want is an old man like Jesus. Do you think I'll ever get one?"

"You better hope not," Mary laughs. "He won't be able to buy you nice things."

"That's okay," Trina says. "We'll just sit in the park and kiss."

Mary snorts and fishes in her clutch for a cigarette and matches.

Margaret bursts through the front door carrying grocery bags and platters, followed by her sons James and Jeff, each of them dragging shopping bags of gifts behind them, the bottoms gaping at the corners, colored paper frayed and cardboard shredding. "Merry Christmas, everybody," Margaret sings out, dropping the bags.

Trina answers, "Merry Christmas, Auntie Margaret."

"Where's John?" asks Mary. "How is he?" She lights her cigarette and holds the match in front of Trina, who blows it out.

"He's with Millie and Will, good as new."

"So much for your maternal instincts," Mary snaps.

Margaret glares at her and leaves the room.

Mary asks the boys, "What do you want for Christmas?"

"We want deviled eggs," Jeff demands.

"Go talk to Grandma," Mary suggests.

"The eggs aren't ready," Trina says. "You might as well go outside."

"Okay," Jeff says, wiping his nose on his sleeve. "One foot off the gutter. Wanna play, Treen?" Without waiting for Trina's answer, the boys run out. Trina feels bad her cousins have no father now and she does. It doesn't seem fair. Margaret unwraps platters of cold fried chicken and deli ham with pineapple and cherries. Still no deviled eggs.

Trina follows her cousins outdoors and stops at the top of the stairs with auntie Maureen and Spizz. They share a crooked little cigarette rolled up in yellow paper. "You're not supposed to sit on the porch," Trina tells them, loyal always to Grandma, caretaker of Trina's dreams. "It's been broken since The Big One. We're gonna fall through if we stay here too long." Trina looks down into the oil-spotted driveway a story below, careful not to lean on the tilting banister.

Maureen and Spizz inhale deeply, then laugh, snorting through their noses like piglets. "You're such a goody two-shoes, Trina. That's why we love you," says Maureen, blowing her niece a smoky kiss.

"She's beautiful," says Spizz.

"I smoked pot before," Trina says. Maureen and Spizz look at each other with big round eyes.

"Sure, you did," says Spizz.

"We're not smoking pot," says Maureen.

A police car pulls up in front of the house. James and Jeff run up the stairs, kicking chips of paint behind them. Their ball bounces against the gutter, forgotten, and jams in front of a tire curbed sharp. Auntie Maureen and Spizz swallow their laughter and cup their hands behind their backs. Uncle Matt sits in the passenger seat, his red afro a bozo beacon beneath the squad car's cherry light.

"Get inside," Maureen tells Trina, and stands up just as Millie and Will pull up behind the police car. Millie holds John on her lap like he's a little baby, even though he's already six.

Trina runs inside to watch from the window. "Auntie Mary, the cops are here."

Mary lunges over, nearly breaking the tree, all soap-opera melodrama, hugging Trina tight. "Don't worry, sweetheart," she says. "Your uncle's just a knucklehead. A big jaybird. A jailbird. Look at that." Mary points outside at all the windows in the houses up and down the street, curtains pulled aside, faces peering out over sprayed-on snow and paper flakes. "Nosy neighbors. Like they never did anything." She squeezes Trina again and calls out, "Mama? Mama! Come out here. It's your only misbegotten juvenile delinquent son." Trina escapes from Mary's arms and goes to the dining room.

Grandma Bunny sets a platter on the buffet. The eggs. "What are you yelling about now, Mary?" Grandma Bunny yells back, winking at Trina.

Trina gazes at the treasured platter. She marvels at their porcelain whites, their fluffy golden yolks, mashed and teased into mayonnaisey clouds. Her fingers tremble. Grandma Bunny nods. For Trina. The first one. Trina pops it whole, exquisite eggy yolkiness squishing out the corners of her mouth. Heaven. Christmas.

The front door opens on Trina's mom carrying John, and behind her, Will, Uncle Matt, and a blue-faced cop. "Well, isn't this a fine Christmas present, Irene," says the cop.

"One second, Reilly." Grandma Bunny turns her attention to her daughter. "How's our little baby John?"

"The doctor says this should do it, Mama. I just wish he would stop crying." Margaret runs out from the dining room to take John from Millie's arms. Trina runs over to kiss her mom.

"Say hello to John, Trina," Millie says. "He's back from the hospital, good as new."

Margaret rocks the baby in her arms, kissing and cooing auntie secrets into his ear. "Yes, you are. Home from the hospital. Home with us."

"He's a cute little feller," the cop says.

"So what is it, Reilly?" Grandma Bunny asks him.

Reilly pulls a Sears Roebuck bag out from behind his back. "Shoplifting. Again."

"It wasn't me! They told me I could keep it because it's for you, Ma," Matt bursts out. Maureen and Spizz come in from the porch on a blast of musk oil and Dentyne.

"I'm ignoring the paperwork on this for the holiday, but he needed an escort home just the same," Reilly continues. "And you're damn lucky it was me and not the other two that got him last time. They want him bad, but seeing as how you're my good friends..."

"Nice wrap job," says Grandma Bunny, putting her hands behind her back so as not to touch the loot.

"Sorry to hear about you and Ned," Reilly says, putting his hand on Grandma's shoulder.

"Open it," Matt yells from his safe spot in the corner of the room, just in case.

Grandma Bunny rubs her palms together, then lays one hand on the little hump on the back of her neck. "Thanks, Reilly," Grandma Bunny says. "How about some egg nog?" Will brings Reilly a drink and Matt puts the Sears Roebuck bag under the tree, then does the funky chicken in the crazy colored lights, singing *"Jingle Bells, Santa smells, Robin laid an egg,"* to Jimi Hendrix air guitar.

"Mama," Mary says. "He should be grounded."

Maureen says, "Mary, you're riding on blame and punishment. Try to forgive our brother, if not for love, then just for the holidays."

Spizz takes Maureen's face in his hands. "That's far out. You're really beautiful, baby." And he kisses Maureen right there. No tongue, from what Trina can make out.

Grandma says, "Unlock it, you two, or take it away and no, Mary, I'm not grounding your brother on Christmas." Matt laughs, an arpeggio of chimpanzee, stadium roar, police-car siren, Woody Woodpecker.

Trina goes back to the buffet and helps herself to another egg. While everyone laughs and screams in the other room, Trina locks herself in the bathroom and sits in the tub, platter before her. She points at the first egg. "I name thee Donder." She stuffs Donder into her mouth and chews him thoroughly. Lord Cupid is next. Then Blixen. She rests. Her throat is full, and she cannot swallow. She gulps in stages, her throat like a snake's, and thinks about how Uncle Matt is her greatest deviled egg lover competition. How last Christmas he ate seven of the dozen. How Auntie Mary didn't even get one. "Thou name is Bartholomew."

She throws Bartholomew into the air and tries to catch him in her open mouth. Not quite, but she eats him anyway. Next are Baby, Max, Phillip, Mighty Mouse. She remembers Uncle Matt got yelled at, but he didn't get in trouble. The last one is King. Sick and satisfied, Trina wonders if she will get in trouble.

James knocks on the bathroom door. Trina climbs out of the tub to let him in.

"Wanna watch me pee?" he asks.

"No, thanks," Trina says. "I'll wait in here." She steps into the shower and pulls the curtain closed.

"What's that doing there?" James looks at the empty platter in the tub while pushing his pants to his knees.

"I ate all the eggs," Trina answers from inside the shower, her nose drying up from the sharp soap smell, listening to James pee in squirts and dribbles.

"You're gonna get it," James says. "I'm finished. Come out."

"Wash your hands," Trina reminds him as she parts the shower curtain and exits like a showgirl, arms in the air. James washes and Trina asks, "Are there any boys in your class like Jesus?"

"What do you mean?" James flexes his arm in the mirror. Nothing.

"Like they do nice things for people and have soft eyes." Trina looks in the mirror. The bow has fallen from her hair, but the goo has kept the hair in place. It feels hard and dry.

"I don't think so."

"Have you ever heard of kissing with your mouth open?"

"HOW?" James looks at her in disbelief, chin hanging down.

"Like Auntie Maureen and her old man. Watch." Trina makes her hand into a fist and places her lips over her forefinger and thumb, sticking her tongue in.

The door handle jiggles. "What are you two doing in there? Unlock the door this instant!" says Auntie Margaret. Trina wipes her kissy hand on her dress and James opens the door. "What have I told you about locking doors?" Little John wails in the front room amid the cooing of all the aunts.

"I peed," says James, "but she didn't watch."

"I ate all the eggs," says Trina.

"James, into the front room right now. Trina, into the bedroom until it's time to open presents." Auntie Margaret returns to screaming John.

Trina flops on the bed. Maureen cradles the phone on her lap and smokes a cigarette, hand out the window in the crisp air, the whites of her eyes bloodshot pink. Maureen points to her tummy and says, "There's an egg in here."

Trina considers this carefully. "But I ate all the eggs."

Maureen takes Trina's hand in hers and places it on her belly mountain. "No, I mean the baby."

"Oh," says Trina, feeling her aunt's belly, which feels just like her own, really. "I knew that. Are you gonna marry Spizz?"

"Maybe. Maybe not." Maureen says, stroking her imaginary protrusion as if it were a pet. "He's going away. To Canada." They close their eyes awhile and Maureen chants *om ma nay pad may om.*

Grandma Bunny knocks on the door. "Time to open presents. Maureen, are you all right?" Maureen smashes out her cigarette and throws the butt out the window. Grandma Bunny sits on the bed and kneads Maureen's shoulders. "Don't mind Mary, you know how she is," Grandma Bunny says. "A baby *is* a miracle." Maureen sighs. "Come on out and watch the kids open presents."

"I guess." Maureen pulls herself up from the bed and brushes her hair in the mirror.

"And you, Miss Trina," Grandma continues. "Shame on you. Eating all the eggs. I hate to do this, but you leave me no choice." She grabs the brush from Maureen's hand. Trina rolls onto her stomach. "How many?" Grandma asks.

"I think three," says Trina, pulling up the back of her dress. Grandma Bunny delivers three swift whacks, three buzzing stings, to Trina's bottom. *We three kings of Orient are,* Trina thinks, as she smiles into the bedspread and a slow tear squeezes out one eye.

"Are you ready to be a good girl?"

"Yes, Grandma." Trina pulls her dress down. It doesn't hurt that bad.

"Give me a kiss then." Trina throws her arms around Grandma Bunny's neck and kisses her cheek. "Okay, let's open the gifts."

Reilly says good-night at the door, rapping Matt playfully on the head with his nightstick, just as Grandpa Ned shows up in a Santa costume with a bag slung over his shoulder. He sips from his flask and he bellows, "roll out the barrel and ho, ho, ho," and everybody laughs. He delivers the gifts all around.

For three and a half minutes, there is much tearing of paper and clapping and wrong sizes and laughing and inappropriate colors. Trina gets polyester Chinese pajamas just like auntie Mary's, a new dress from her mom, and a doll with hair that grows from Grandma Bunny, who wears her new Sears Roebuck apron that reads "To heck with housework, let's go watch the Giants play." The boys all get new pajamas and Hot Wheels. Matt gets a skateboard. Millie holds hands with Will. Margaret holds John in her lap. John cries and cries and cries while the kids all change into their new stiff pajamas.

At midnight, everyone stands in front of the television and sings: *Silent night, holy night.*

All is calm.

"Not around here," Grandma Bunny says under her breath.

All is bright. 'Round yon virgin,

Margaret digs her elbow into Mary's ribs. Mary pinches her sister on the pale fleshy inside of her upper arm.

Mother and child.

Holy infant so tender and mild.

Sleep in heavenly peeeeeeeace,

Matt sings 'peace' like an opera singer, holding the note for eight Mississippis. James sings 'pee' under his breath to Trina and mashes her toe with his.

Slee-eep in heavenly peace.

"Amen!" booms Grandpa Ned.

Jeff places Baby Jesus into the manger. Auntie Maureen leans over Trina and whispers, "Jesus was a love child, you know. I'll have a love child, too. Her name will be Jennifer Juniper."

Millie and Will squeeze Trina around the shoulders, the three of them all connected again somehow.

Trina closes her eyes and flies far above the room in her Chinese pants, arms spread, cheeks full and smiling against the rushing Christmas air. She turns tight looping somersaults, then extends her body like a knife, swooping dangerously close to the cold metal tree, twisting and glittering, fishy between the multi-colored lights. She hovers above her family as they hold hands and pray together. Trina opens her eyes and prays to them, to their spirit and their love. She prays for her love-child cousin. She prays for Pocahontas braids and an old man like Jesus. She prays that her brother can poop of his own free will. She flies higher and harder than ever, knowing that this might be her very last chance, no hands not touching nothing.

BADASS

· · · · ·

James Monroe had a sperm on the inside of his left sneaker. A blue-inked cartoon sperm with skinny legs, a hang-tongue grin, and the name "Sammy" written in flames along his whiplash tail. James Monroe had joined homeroom when classes began last week. He slumped at his desk in his Derby jacket and dirty jeans, fingering a zit on the back of his neck, sentenced to a year of torture repeating seventh grade.

Across the aisle, Evie Moulton felt Sammy's pop-eyed leer as she dutifully translated irregular verbs on this morning's surprise quiz. *Estar—to be. Saber—to know. Sentir—to feel.* This new proximity to James Monroe made Evie feel as though she somehow possessed him. As though she all at once knew him, the same way she'd suddenly cottoned to Spanish, its singsong words zinging into her brain when she least expected.

James Monroe tossed his shoulder-length hair across his right shoulder with a twitch of his neck. So many shades of black—some shone silver!—swooped across his forehead in a deliberate wave. He cut his eyes, *sus ojos*, at her paper, and the protective wall of Evie's arm fell open, softening its curve, as though it obeyed some silent "open sesame" without Evie having any part of it. Evie was shocked by this; she had never cheated on a quiz before. But something in her responded to James

Monroe in a way that was unexplainable, unstoppable. She finished the quiz easily, the answers flying out of her fingers like lightening, her brain in a fever.

In the seven years since Evie had been at that school, she had never spoken to James Monroe. Suddenly, Evie began to sketch, in the top right corner of her notebook, Tammy the cartoon *girl* sperm. Tammy had Pocahontas braids (like Evie's), flirty eyelashes (like Evie would have as soon as she was allowed to wear makeup) and a T-shirt with a fat heart on it like the one Evie wore today. She left the notebook splayed open, pages waterfalling into the aisle, its college-ruled gridlines exposed. A person would have to say something.

So engrossed in Tammy was Evie that she hadn't noticed their teacher swoosh past to the door in the back of the room. Had no idea Labarber was conferring with Hertzberg, the counselor, until she was heard clearing her goiter. "People, let us welcome a new girl to class. Alison Malashenko," she read from the slip. "She's transferred from Crestmoor." Labarber arched a drawn-on eyebrow to underline what everyone already knew: crap school. *"Buenos días, Alison. Me llamo Señora Labarber."* She trilled her name and pointed to its perfect Palmer shape in an upper corner of the blackboard.

Alison wore obvious hand-me-downs: too-short low-rider jeans, a boy's flannel shirt tied above her navel, scuffed platform sandals with an extra inch between her heel and their loose straps. But she twirled her thin yellow ponytail with one index finger as though she liked herself exactly that way. *"Muchas gracias,"* Alison smirked.

Everyone in class giggled. Everyone, Evie noticed, except James Monroe, who seemed mesmerized by the J he was now carving into his desk with a penknife.

"Estudiamos verbos irregulares. Do you know any irregular verbs, *Señorita* Malashenko?" Labarber asked, not one to tolerate smirkiness or giggling.

"Labarber?" Alison responded with an exaggerated accent, and slipped into the empty desk on the opposite side of James Monroe.

A few people snickered, and the end of homeroom bell shrieked. Before Evie could even finish angling Tammy the girl sperm in James Monroe's direction, the other students jumped to their feet, slammed books closed and herded into the corridor. The room was empty in seconds except for the new girl and *Señora* Labarber, who suggested Evie help Alison finder her locker and show her the way to her next class.

· · · · ·

It was Norma Parsons' fault Evie had to spend her lunch period with Alison: Norma was home with the chicken pox under strict quarantine. Which had been fine with Evie. It allowed her to spend lunch periods blissfully alone in the library, flipping through art books. Evie was especially fond of Botticelli's Birth of Venus, not just because of Venus' obvious modest beauty, but because of the intricate tangle of limbs borne by the winged creatures who threw flowers at the object of their desire. But today Evie felt duty bound to share her lunch hour with Alison. They sat cross-legged in the grass at the lower field, near the pine trees at the far end of the track.

"Let's trade," Alison asked first thing, thrusting her brown bag at Evie.

"Why?" Evie had never considered swapping her lunch, but now that it was offered, she couldn't think of a single thing she liked about the lunches that were packed for her each day. White bread. Crusts (never cut off, like Mrs. Parsons did for Norma, who claimed she had sensitive gums just to mess with her mom). Lunch meat plus spread. The occasional PB&J. Dried out carrot sticks or celery. A Chip Ahoy. Boredom in a bag.

"Why not?" Alison retorted. "You might get to experience the most delicious sandwich in the entire universe. Or not." She swung her bag back and forth like a pendulum in front of Evie's eyes. "If you hate it, we'll switch back. I promise."

Before Evie's lips could form the word "no," Alison's bag was in her hands; her own bag had been snatched away. Alison quickly unwrapped and inspected Evie's offerings. "Mmm," she said, her moth full of what Evie knew was slightly stale bread and greasy salami. "Delicious."

Evie unwrapped the surprise sandwich more slowly, inspecting the lumpy slices of white bread. "What is this?"

"Just taste it." Alison wolfed down the rest of Evie's sandwich, crumpled the clear plastic wrap and burped.

"I guess I better like it now, right?" Evie couldn't believe how easily she had ended up without a back-up sandwich.

"You'll love it." Alison swung her ponytail over her shoulder and stroked it with both hands as though it were a mink stole. "Natalie made it special for my first day."

"Who's Natalie?" Evie opened the sandwich like a book, trying to identify its mysterious guts. "Watermelon jelly?" she guessed. "Papaya jam?" She put her nose to the pink stuff. "It smells like fish," she said. Venus was a salt creature, borne of ocean brine.

"It's butter. And Natalie's my mother. A.K.A. Mrs. Malashenko." Alison said, shoving carrot sticks into her mouth.

Evie pinched her nose and bit, exploring the mouthful with her tongue before daring to chew. The spongy white bread was familiar enough. And there was no such thing as too much butter. She rolled small, velvety beads along her tongue, then pressed them against her upper palate until they popped. Her mouth filled with miniature explosions of salt and fish and seawater. Evie gave a snort of surprise, and launched a pink globe from her nose onto the napkin on her lap.

"Flying caviar!" Alison threw her head back and shrieked, followed by a cackling giggle that ended in *hyaw-hyaw-hyaw*.

Evie couldn't help herself; she joined in Alison's ridiculous laugh, making two birds flutter in panic from the stand of pines, which made the girls laugh more.

"You should come over to my house after school!" Alison cried out.

"I can't," Evie said, as she scarfed down her caviar sandwich. "I have Debate Club on Tuesdays," although as she said it, she remembered that Mrs. Parsons, whose turn it was to drive the carpool, was under quarantine of Norma's pox.

"Debate Club? How lame." Alison shrugged. "Your loss."

With that gesture, Alison became something better, something brighter than any girl Evie had ever met. As if she knew how to grab handfuls of starlight and sprinkle it all over herself. She gave Evie her address just in case.

· · · · ·

Evie shouldered her book bag and jammed her hands in the pockets of her pea coat as she headed toward Cunningham Lane. Evie had been driven down these streets on the way to the mall and to the doctor's and dentist's offices, but Evie had never walked them alone before. This new point of view fascinated Evie: the close-up on barking dogs and younger kids playing Serial Killer and Roller Queen on the street. They stopped yelling and stared at her as she approached, then resumed hollering after she passed.

Alison's house needed a paint job. The front yard was mostly dirt. No matter how many times Evie pressed it, the doorbell didn't work.

Alison flung open the door. "Hello, darling," she said, posing with one arm up along the door jamb. She wore a shiny green cocktail dress and spike-heeled shoes. "How divine of you to visit." She screamed, and pulled Evie inside.

Evie was overwhelmed by the strangeness of Alison's house, so different from the Parsons' beige worsteds and knitted afghans or the shabby velvets and worn carpets of her own home. She followed Alison down a shadowy hall, past cartons stamped "Romanoff Caviar," catching whiffs of perfume, cigarette smoke and old meat, then into a grown-up's bedroom. Evie retreated quickly, stepping back behind the threshold. From what she could see—the heavy brocade drapes were pulled tight—the walls were light peach, the drapes and bedspread dark blue. Scarves were draped over lampshades and mirrors, of which there were many. "Come on," Alison grabbed Evie's wrist and slung her toward the large bed, onto which Evie fell and from where she watched Alison slam dresses down the rod from one end of the wall-length closet to the other. "No, no, no, no, no," Alison said, stopping occasionally to regard a dress, then Evie.

"Oh, hold the phone. This one's you all over." Alison held a dress high, its blousy top a wisp of white see-through fabric, its light blue skirt cascading in petal-like layers. "The lotus blossom." She tossed it at Evie. "I got falsies on. What do you think?" Alison cupped her breasts. "There's more. Here, try some." She rummaged through a drawer and threw a handful of brassieres onto the bed. They were silken contraptions smelling of powder and sweat. Evie flinched when one of the straps hit her leg, but she couldn't stop herself from reaching out to pinch the stitched padded lace on the cups. And the colors! Magenta, sapphire, chocolate, black. Nothing like the dingy cosseting that hung in the laundry room every weekend. "Where's your mom?" Evie asked.

"Work." Alison unzipped the cocktail dress, hurled it to the floor, and jackknifed her way into another. Evie changed clothes with girls in P.E. all the time, but it was different with these grown-up smells and clothes and the bed and the new girl before her. "Hell's bells, where are my manners?" Alison ran from the room, and Evie took the opportunity to strip off her clothes and pull on the blue bra and the lotus blossom dress. She stood on the bed and looked at herself in the mirror, arms stuck out in a T. The effect was far from glamorous, but if she wrapped her braids around her head and squinted her eyes, Evie could imagine the catalog model she might someday become.

Alison returned with caviar on crackers, a cigarette and a beer. "I wasn't sure how cool you were, but just in case," she pointed to the beer. "That dress looks bitchin' on you. It brings out your brown eyes and your brown hair and everything." Alison put a cigarette in her mouth and picked up a statue of a gold cat. She flicked the cat's ear and a flame appeared on the top of its head, from which she lit her cigarette. "I love menthol. Don't you?"

"I don't smoke." Evie jumped on the bed, landed on her butt, and bounced onto Alison, who hugged Evie against her and laughed. *Hyaw-hyaw-hyaw.*

"Here," Alison handed the cigarette to Evie. "You need some shoes."

Evie practiced posing with the cigarette then finally put the filter end of it in her mouth. Nothing happened. "That wasn't so bad."

"You have to suck it," Alison said. She took the cigarette, demonstrated and handed it back to Evie.

Alison looked so sophisticated. She wasn't dying or anything. Evie sucked the cigarette this time. Columns of smoke slithered skyward, teasing her eyes, her nose.

"That looks so badass," Alison said. "Do it again."

Evie obeyed. Her mouth filled with smoke and the salty memory of caviar. A vision of slimy fish eyes appeared. "I think I'm going to barf."

Evie ignored the bright copper hairs around the rim as she gagged over the toilet, her eyes streaming tears. When nothing came up, she removed the dress quickly and regarded herself in the mirror. There was no starlight around her, only red-rimmed eyes and screwy braids.

When Evie came out of the bathroom, Alison was propped up on the bed pillows, wearing a lacy brassiere. She patted the spot next to her. Evie crawled onto the bed with arms and legs shaking, then noticed her book bag unzipped next to Alison, her notebook wide open on Alison's lap. "What are you doing?" Evie cried, lunging weakly at Alison, who fended her off easily with one arm.

"She's bitchin'," Alison said, pointing to Tammy the sperm. "Did you make her up?"

"Yes. No. Kind of." Evie sunk back into the sleep-scented pillow and drew the comforter around her. "You know that boy that sits between us in homeroom? James Monroe?" Her voice trembled as she spoke his name. She coughed to hide it.

"You like Jim!" Alison's hypnotic eyes lasered in on Evie's; her lips curved into a cunning smile, as though they'd just devoured something young and delicious.

Jim? *Jim?* The syllable bounced around Evie's brain, its presumed intimacy more than she could bear. Ever since always, James Monroe was James Monroe. But after one day, Alison called him Jim, as though she had a permission slip to say the name of any old person she wanted. A green leaf of tangled emotion unfurled inside Evie.

"He looks like a badass," Alison continued. "Like my boyfriend at my old school, only not as cute."

"Probably not as smart either," Evie said, instantly guilty for betraying James Monroe. Evie wondered how to make Alison see what she saw. Oh, why did she even care what Alison thought?

"See! You do so like him! I knew it. Tell me everything!" Alison pushed the notebook aside and stroked Evie's arm. "I'll be your best friend ever. I promise," she crooned.

Norma Parson had been Evie's best friend until now and even she bugged Evie more often than not. *Best friends have to prove themselves before they become that,* Evie thought. *Pass a test. Rip something off. At least keep a secret.* Evie had told no one of her feelings for James Monroe. Not Norma, not even her diary. She worried if she were to put them into words, her feelings might become something else. Real. Or tarnished. Or too shiny to remain hers alone. Evie was suddenly overcome by the unreal reality of two girls in grown-up lingerie in bed. To know what was right and yet do what was wrong left Evie buoyant, like a balloon flying ever higher on a thrusting wind. She felt brazen and raw as she recounted James Monroe's troubled history.

From slugging the principal on the first day of kindergarten until Valentine's Day last winter, when he just stopped showing up. There'd been plenty of stories about James Monroe's *Ripley's Believe It Or Not!* family life: Mrs. Monroe jumped ship and left the three boys with their dad. James spent a week with some richies before getting kicked out, he put in an appearance at Juvie, visited the ER after an overdose of Darvon. These stories punched Evie right in the heart, and she told Alison so as she ended with, "Ever since James Monroe started sitting next to me, I feel different. Like I can't breathe and my blood burns and my heart flies around."

Alison wound a section of hair around one finger. "You ever talk to him?"

"No way!" Evie said, shuddering in fear and delight at the prospect. "I thought if he saw Tammy, he would know…." Her voice trailed away. As soon as she said the words, she knew they were stupid.

"Boys don't care about pictures of sperm, not even cute sperm," Alison said. "They just want to know you might let them do something to you. Then they'll do anything you want. Just leave it up to me." She kissed Evie on the cheek and tore the Tammy page from Evie's notebook. "You'll have Jimboy's tongue down your throat in no time."

■ ■ ■ ■ ■

Evie bulldozed meatloaf around on her plate creating a mountain landscape with green beans for trees. She wondered what the world looked like before there were mountains, before trees. She wondered if Venus was cold without any clothes on; it was often foggy at the beach. She wondered what Alison was going to say to James Monroe.

Evie's father, The Nose, was interested in everything Evie did. "What kind of mess are you making there, Ever?" "Ever" was her real name; she would never forgive her parents for that.

"Art," she replied, picking at a mountain top.

"Did you learn anything in school today?" Evie's mother, The Mouth, always backed up The Nose. She casually cubed her meat loaf.

"This new girl brought a caviar sandwich, and I had to eat it." Evie flattened her mashed potatoes into an alpine lake. "Plus she said she would be my best friend on her very first day of school. Don't you think that's bogus?"

"Bogus indeed," The Nose agreed. "How was Debate Club?"

"Fine." Evie scarfed the trees.

"Are you sure?" The Mouth asked this slowly, deliberately, between chews.

"Positive." Evie lied. "Norma farted right in the middle of her rebuttal." She debuted a high-pitched shriek ending in Alison's signature *hyaw-hyaw-hyaw*.

"What was *that?*" The Mouth looked up in alarm. "Honey, are you okay?"

The Nose slapped his hands on the table. "What have we said about lying?"

"Don't," Evie sighed. *How did he know?*

"And smoking?" The Nose folded his hands into a steeple. He was serious.

Evie said nothing and wished she'd accepted the cologne spritz Alison had offered as Evie ran out the door.

"You're on restriction," said The Mouth, sipping her white wine.

"No going to the park for two weeks," said The Nose.

Evie wondered what James Monroe was doing *right now.*

■ ■ ■ ■ ■

The Nose had warned of the dangers of gum since the first time Evie bit into a powdery pink rectangle of double-barrel Bazooka. If swallowed, gum could lodge in her esophagus, stick to her ribs, inflate in her lungs or clog up her colon.

But swallow was what Evie did when she saw Alison talking to James Monroe in the Great Court the next morning before school. Alison was waving her arms around like some kind of octopus, and her crayon-colored bangles clacked as they slid up and down her tentacles, tentacles whose tiny white hairs glinted in the weak sun that shone on Alison alone. The hard pink wad lodged itself in Evie's tonsils, which would now probably have to come out.

James Monroe smoothed back his greasy bangs, exposing his face, with its purple shadows, sharp planes and pink spots. He squinted into Alison's spotlight, and then something incredible happened: the corners of his lips curled up, creating something like a smile. Neither big nor wide, it actually looked a bit painful, like a pleased grimace. His stained, crooked teeth revealed themselves in a friendly, come-out-and-play way.

It was a miracle, one of the most beautiful things Evie had ever seen. Her breath tried to jump into her mouth, but her gum was still tonsil-bound, and what erupted sounded like a weird trumpet blast, mouth flatulence, an out-of-tune pig.

James Monroe looked Evie's way. *His eyes were blue. Azul.* Alison and her bangles melted away into the ringing of a beautiful bell that called them to heavenly homeroom.

■ ■ ■ ■ ■

Respirar—to breathe. Abatir—to knock down (overthrow). Transformar—to change. Evie's brain swirled around transitive verbs, her thoughts smooth and creamy and delicious like strawberry ice cream. Did Alison introduce James Monroe to Tammy? Did she tell him how Evie felt? Evie couldn't wait to corner Alison at lunch and find out what she said. But instead of running to the lunch circle at the end of P.E., she lingered over changing back into her street clothes, as if she couldn't bear to surrender the pleasure of her fantasy of what was said, of not knowing. Once she knew what Alison said, Evie's world would be exactly the same and entirely different.

Lunch period was almost over by the time Evie reached the trees. "What happened?" Alison called out. "I was starving. I had to eat my own sandwich."

Evie shrugged and sat down on the grass to unwrap her sandwich.

"That's OK." Alison thrust a plastic sack at her. "This is for you."

Evie pulled out a red silk scarf and a Jolly Rancher candy. "What for?"

"For fun." Alison batted Evie's sandwich from her hands. "Pay attention." She grabbed the scarf and tied it around Evie's eyes, then shifted so she was sitting behind her.

The darkness suffused with light reminded Evie of the summer she was reigning champ at Helen Keller Kickball. The candy wrap crackled as Alison opened it. The scent of watermelon washed the air around Evie.

"Pull up your shirt," Alison commanded.

"What? No!" Evie said, but did nothing as she felt Alison's cold hands pull up her turtleneck. She shivered at the wind's tingly brush. The skin on her back went to gooseflesh. She felt something warm. Alison was moving her finger on Evie's back, making a large swoop, then a straight line, then a series of up-and-down lines. "What's that?" Evie asked.

"It's the name of the boy who invited us over to his house after school," Alison said. "I wrote it in Jolly Rancher spit for good luck."

"What?" Evie repeated dumbly. She didn't understand anything that was happening. Not her shirt being up, not Alison touching her, not the words that were coming from Alison's mouth, not what was being written on a piece of her body that preferred to be covered in fabric.

"God, what's wrong with you?" Alison sounded exasperated. "I said Jim wants us to come over to his house after school."

"Who?" Evie asked. She didn't know any Jims.

"Jim, you ninny. Your boyfriend?" Alison tore the scarf from Evie's eyes. "God, try to make things interesting around here and you go all retarded."

"Shut up," Evie said. "I couldn't hear you." She finally breathed. "Did you tell him I like him?"

"Maybe," Alison taunted. "Maybe not."

They were invited to James Monroe's house, only Alison called him Jim. Evie's mind went blank and dark; there was rumbling like thunder in the back of her brain. "I have to go home now," Evie whispered. She leapt to her feet, stumbled, and then righted herself without thinking, as if a hand from the sky pulled her up by the scruff. She churned across the field and out onto the street, floating over herself, watching herself run. She was at her front door before she realized she'd left her book bag and lunch behind. There were grass stains on both knees.

"What are you doing home?" The Mouth asked when she came into the kitchen and found Evie pouring milk on a bowl of cereal.

"I don't feel good." She shoveled cereal into her face.

"What's the matter?"

"I have a stomach ache."

"Then you shouldn't be having cereal."

"A headache too."

"Do you have a fever?" The Mouth put her hand to Evie's forehead. "You're not hot at all."

"Don't touch me!" Evie said, whipping her head back and knocking her bowl so milk and cereal sloshed over the sides. "Now see what you made me do!"

"Just because you're sick doesn't mean you can be fresh," The Mouth said. "After you clean up that mess, you can stay in your room till dinnertime."

Evie did as she was told with no further argument and went to her room. She took a three-hour nap like she used to when she was little. When she woke up, she climbed out the window, wondering what the inside of James Monroe's house looked like.

· · · · ·

Evie and Alison walked without talking down Oakdale Street. It was only two blocks away from Alison's house, but the neighborhood was much worse. The yards here were squared off with cyclone fences. Some had bars with spikes on top or barbed wire. One ramshackle palace up at the corner had a crumbling column topped with a jumble of scuffed tennis shoes next to a rusted, filigreed gate. "That's the one," Alison said. "642."

Evie blinked one eye at a time, watching the house jump back and forth, like an old-time cartoon strip. A dying shrub. A dented mailbox.

A front door peeling pink paint. A dirt path alongside the garage. A dog somewhere barked, and both girls jumped.

Evie pushed open the front gate and started up the white rock path to the front door, but Alison grabbed her. "No," she whispered. "He said for you to go around back." She pulled Evie up the drive and along the side of the house until they came to a gate. Alison unhooked the latch and pushed open the door.

"Go," said Evie.

"You go," Alison shot back. "You're the one who likes him. I'll wait here."

Evie felt as though she were floating two inches above the ground. She looked back a couple times to see Alison standing there, smiling and waving her on.

Later, Alison would be able to recall how she got to the middle of the back yard, which was just a bunch of uneven cement. She didn't recall moving her legs or thinking she might be trespassing or whatever anyone might call it. But she did remember the next part, as clearly as though in a dream.

James Monroe was standing in the dining room of his crummy house. His hands were pressed against the wall, like what TV cops made bad guys do. His shirt was off. His pants were down. There was a man with him, Evie guessed it was his father, who looked like an opposite centaur. His strong, compact body carried a large animal head, where unkempt gray hair stood on end, forming big donkey ears. Old man Monroe's arm was raised, his hand cocked back and high, a length of brown leather curled up in the air like a jumping snake.

James Monroe was looking down at the floor, the side of his face hidden by that familiar swag of hair. Ribs ridged his torso. The buttocks were round. Cupid-like. His leg muscles were rigid and faintly pink, and the slant of his right thigh hid whatever was between his long, skinny legs. Sammy the sperm's skinny legs flashed into Evie's brain, quickly erased. James Monroe's skin was like glow-in-the-dark milk. Like skin Evie had only seen on a postcard of a Roman statue called David. "Study hard," The Mouth had said when she stuck the card on their fridge with a magnet. "And maybe you'll get to see something beautiful like that someday."

Evie was amazed to see her reflection there in the glass, between the donkey man and James Monroe. She floated there like a ghost in her striped T-shirt and jeans. She would take the blows for him.

The donkey man shouted and looked directly at Evie. He smiled and put all he had into his arm.

Evie dashed back to the side of the house, but Alison was gone. The door was shut, the latch hooked again. Evie could hear faint yelling from inside as she fumbled the latch again and again. Where was Alison? She ran all the way home with images of James Monroe flashing through her mind. His sweatpants pushed down and pooled around his ankles, one pink sock sprouting from all that inside-out gray. The image throbbed, shocking her over and over with its electrical, fluorescent pulse. Evie wondered if it was possible to get belt-beat to death and imagined strips of hanging skin and streaks of blood covering James Monroe's glowing body.

When Evie climbed through her bedroom window, The Nose was sitting on her bed, waiting. "Daddy!" She clambered over the sill and ran to him, throwing her arms around him and covering his face with kisses.

"What was that for?" her father asked, rubbing his cheek. "You're in a heap of trouble, young lady."

"I know," Evie said. "I shouldn't have left the house. Whatever punishment you think is right I'll do. I promise never to disobey again."

The pink sock stayed glued to Evie's mind all through dinner. She wondered where Alison had gone, and hoped she was all right. Later it occurred to her that Alison might have made up James Monroe's invitation, but Evie wasn't angry. She was more sad to lose a best friend in a day. She wondered what James Monroe had done to deserve what she saw. Evie had a pink sock of her own, and she had an idea.

■ ■ ■ ■ ■

The next morning, Evie walked to school in measured strides. The blue sock on her left foot merely moved her body forward. The pink one on her right drew her closer to James Monroe. "Crap on Alison," she said. Evie looked around, horrified, realizing in a slow-motion bubble of awareness she had spoken out loud. *Double crap!* She pretended not to care and stopped to admire an enormous orange bloom at the corner yard. Evie couldn't remember the Spanish word for beautiful, so she picked one that rhymed instead. *Rosa peligrosa.* Evie checked for bees and pressed her face into its center, then ripped off all the petals and stuffed them in her pocket. Evie ran the rest of the way to school. Left, right. Blue, pink. Left, right. One foot magic, the other light.

Sorprenderse—to be surprised. Arreglarse—to get ready. Despedirse—to say goodbye to. James Monroe's empty desk separated Alison and Evie that morning. While Labarber conjugated reflexive verbs and Alison kept her head down, Evie stared at the scraggly pine outside the window. At the tip of each arm were soft budlets of new growth in a glowy green distinct from its longer darker needles. Evie closed her eyes and pictured a place to sleep. She had hardly slept at all the previous night; James Monroe's skin had kept her awake.

There was a hill below the fort in Buckeye Park where Evie used to go when she was a kid. The hill was covered in sour grass you could doze in and suck on at the same time. She didn't believe the grass was sour because dogs peed on it, no matter what Norma said. Under a glade of buckeyes was a small protected pad where deer came to sleep at night. She loved the earthy hammocks of long matted grass. Evie would take a sleeping bag, a Snickers, her notebook and a pencil. She thought about the naps she had taken there, the sun burning rainbow rings into the insides of her eyes and her cheeks warm even as wind whipped through the grass. If James Monroe had bruises she would cut her flannel P.J.s into squares and tape them over the purple spots. If his arm was broken she would knit daisy chains, miles of them, and wrap them around his arm like a cast. If the belt buckle cut into his skin, she would lick off the blood to make it clean and spray the open wounds with Bactine. She would tell him she loved him no matter what he did, no matter how wrong. She would remind him he could be forgiven or start over.

"Evie Moulton!" A ruler slapped Evie's desk. Labarber waggled a quarter sheet of ditto paper in front of Evie's face. "Maybe you'd like to sleep through detention, because that's where you're going to spend lunch."

"Ooh, badass," Alison whispered, but Evie refused to look her way.

■ ■ ■ ■ ■

Evie entered the library at three fifteen, the designated detention time. She threw down her book bag and slumped in a wooden chair, waiting for a teacher to show.

The clock leaned into 3:25, and still no one came. Evie fished a stick of gum from a side pocket in her pack and slid a book off the nearby shelf: "Mystery of Atlantis." She opened the book to see who'd checked it out. Her heart thudded so hard at the name on the manila pocket it was like she'd been socked in the chest. James Monroe had touched this book, taken it home, possibly to bed to read with a flashlight under the covers through the night. She flipped through the pages, stopping at an illustration of pink buildings with Roman-style columns underwater, wrapped in silky strands of kelp and sea grass. The front door clunked open. Evie shoved the book into the unzipped mouth of her bag.

"So, Moulton," Hertzberg said, hopping onto the library counter and crossing his legs Indian-style. "What're you in for?"

"Good behavior," Evie said, thinking of all the names she'd never scratched into the walls of bathroom stalls, the textbook pages she'd never marked with non-existent boyfriends' initials, the times she hadn't been late to class because she'd been in the parking lot puffing on menthols.

"This your first time?"

Badass Evie said, "Yeeeaaaah," drawing out the single syllable to three. "What am I supposed to do in here anyway?" She dug into the wad of gum with her index finger, stretched it out long and whipped out her finger, watching with satisfaction as the gum whirled around her finger like a Maypole streamer.

"Whatever you want as long as you don't chew gum." Hertzberg pointed at the trash.

Evie walked across the room to toss her gum. By the time she sat down again, Hertzberg had cracked a can of root beer. Evie pulled out "Mystery of Atlantis," eager to absorb the same words James Monroe had in his head.

The text was stilted and difficult to comprehend, with phrases like "Galactic Confederation" and "Brothers of Light." There was something about a city inside the earth, and another city that was orbiting the earth and fell into the sea. Evie wondered what color the sky was at Buckeye Park, and whether the leaves that had started to change green to red had begun to fall to the ground. She turned to another page. "Once upon a time all Peoples knew all Secrets of Creation because they lived in Harmony with the Higher Laws and Spirit of their Souls." She admired the sentence for a long while, then tore a strip of paper from her notebook and, in her best writing, copied the sentence and put the paper in her pea coat pocket.

At four o'clock, Hertzberg lobbed his empty soda can into the trash and slammed his briefcase shut. "Scram," he said.

"I thought detention was an hour," she said, then sighed. Being a badass was not her basic instinct.

Hertzberg's tongue tucked his mustache into the corners of his mouth. "I don't want to see you in here anymore. Now get out."

The wind tossed Evie's braids as she crossed the upper field toward home. The tall pine branches whirled like crazy people arms. Ice plant crunched and broke beneath her feet as she short-cutted to the lower field. She was going to give James Monroe his fortune. That would break the ice. *Once upon a time all Peoples knew all Secrets of Creation...*

"Evie!" Someone—guess who?—was waiting at the gate Evie had to go through to get home. Evie didn't want to talk to Alison, but she'd look stupid if she turned around. Plus she'd have to go back through the whole school and go all the way around if she did. It was already late. *Crap on Alison.* Evie slowed her walk and listened to the jagged sounds of her breath. The pink sock warmed her foot. By the time she reached the gate, her breathing was even. She smoothed out her braids.

"Look what Jim gave me," Alison said. She tossed her ponytail so the blond streaks caught the fogshine. In her palm was a small suede bag decorated with beads and fringe.

"What's that?" Evie asked. "Looks like some damn Indian crap to me."

Alison gave Evie a strange look. Part hurt kitten, part respect. With a dramatic flourish, Alison shook something from the bag into her palm, then closed her fist. Her smile was silly with gloat. "Guess."

"I don't care what it is," Evie said, and stepped backwards to remove herself from Alison's power.

In painstaking slow motion, Alison's fingers bloomed open, revealing a small red-brown circle in the center of her palm. Beams of light and white heat seemed to emanate from the small, dime-sized disc.

Alison's chest rose and sank with an emphatic breath. "I went back to Jim's house after you left yesterday."

"And?" Evie started to sweat again. Her pits. Her legs. Her chest.

"First we started talking about you, but then we started making out. I don't know how it happened, but he fingered me for like fifteen minutes. It was practically rape." Alison had a weird kind of smile as she said it.

"So what is that?" Evie asked.

"Duh, silly." Alison tossed her ponytail. "It's my hymen! He popped my cherry."

Evie wasn't sure that could be true, but she wasn't sure it couldn't. Either way, it was terrifying. Her insides crumbled into a pile of sand. "What are you going to do with it?" Her voice was hoarse.

Alison looked straight at Evie. "I'm taking it to Hertzberg. Jim is going to get in so much trouble. He'll probably be expelled."

"Why?"

"I told him you liked him, but he put the moves on me," Alison said. "He deserves it."

"You're an evil slut," Evie said. "We're not friends anymore." She pushed Alison out of the way and bolted through the gate.

"I thought you'd be happy for me," she heard Alison cry as she ran down the street.

Evie undressed and went to bed when she got home that afternoon. She didn't know *what* she was supposed to feel. Sometimes her arms and legs were made of wood, other times there was buzzing in her ears. Her stomach joined the gymnastics team, and her thoughts went so fast she couldn't catch them. Almost as if her body were only one part of her and the rest of her, the invisible parts, hovered outside of her, outside her house, somewhere far away, deep underground or circling around planet Earth. It didn't even help when The Mouth brought her soup.

· · · · ·

Evie had a headache all through homeroom the next day, but she was determined to deliver her message to James Monroe. James Monroe looked exactly the way he always did. He sucked on a Tootsie Pop, slumped at his desk, Derby jacket zipped up to his chin. Alison's ponytail was unwashed and limp, its blond streaks turned pale chlorine green. Labarber read a story aloud. *Una historia.* Notebooks began to slam shut thirty seconds before the bell.

Evie calibrated her movements—pull up white knee-highs, smear green apple-scented gloss across lips, smudge sticky finger on inside hem of skirt, extract James Monroe's fortune from pocket of pea coat. It was covered in wrinkled rose petals.

Señora Labarber made an announcement: "Mr. Monroe, please report to the counselor's office."

When the bell rang, James Monroe sprang to his feet, whipped off his jacket, and kicked his desk sideways, hard. Its metal feet groaned across the linoleum, knocking the desks in front and behind out of alignment.

Evie leaned across to pull the desks back into place.

"No!" he said, his voice a strange lowing, a bellow, that seemed to burst from his belly. He used both hands to shove the desk harder this time. The crooked line of desks folded in on itself like a train off its track, jamming into Alison.

"What the hell!" she exclaimed, doubling over from the impact of a table into her midsection. "What a jerk!" she said, meeting Evie's eyes. "You're a jerk," she yelled after him, but James Monroe was already in the corridor, hooting like a beastly night owl.

Evie became very still and felt a blurry wave curling up the base of her spine. *Shoosh!* It caved in on itself as she walked faster to separate herself from Alison.

Shoosh! The wave rolled up Evie's spine and crashed at her waist as she entered the crowded hall.

James Monroe was at his locker in the Great Court. Pulling out books, a tennis shoe, loose papers, tossing them to the ground, winding up and pitching a half-skinned softball in a mean, fast arc.

"Heads," somebody yelled. "Monroe's going mental."

The Science Lab window shattered, raining glass into the planter box below.

More papers flew from James Monroe's locker. Bumper stickers, detention slips, mimeographed sheets. By the time Evie joined him, a third wave was breaking across her shoulders.

James Monroe's cheeks were stained red, his breath blew in fast puffs.

Evie put her hand on the combination dial; its metal ridges were cold. He was so beautiful right now. So wild.

James Monroe turned his head slowly to look at her, his snake eyes pinning the tide on her shore. "What do you want?" he hissed.

"I wanted to tell you about Atlantis," Evie had planned to say. "How I knew you when we were both fish. How I wore the pink sock so you'd know. I know you," she thought as loud as she could. "I really do." But nothing came out of her glossy, apple-scented mouth, her betrayer's lips, *nothing*.

She pressed the folded, flower-daubed paper into his hand. He looked down at it, then back up at Evie. She searched for the crack of doom in his eyes but saw something else. Something that glittered, something that begged. Like words to a song she knew.

James Monroe raised his penknife's dirty blade to her throat. "I want to rape you."

"Monroe!" Hertzberg was suddenly there. "It's over! Right now."

· · · · ·

Buckeye Park was deserted by the time Evie arrived, close to five. All the kids, dogs, teams and scout troops that usually jammed the small flat area below the acres of overgrown hiking trails had already dispersed, leaving behind soda cans, a girls' white blouse size 6X and trampled, flat lawn. The streetlamps' electric lights were just coming on, their faint pink blush shy against the fog's darkening slant. It was strange to be there alone. She had the feeling she was being watched, like she was in a movie.

Evie hurried around the park's perimeter and ducked onto trail number three. Ran halfway to the top of Buckeye Mountain, to her place. She rolled out her sleeping bag in the deer's pillowy nest and breathed in their sharp animal tang. Peeled back the Snickers wrapper and opened "Mystery of Atlantis" to a random page:

The Masters of Wisdom warned of a Great Catastrophe in order to act as Light Bearers to Mankind on its Journey of Forgetting. When Love, Wisdom and Power were reunited, the Masters would return to establish a New School of Wisdom.

Evie rolled over onto her back, using the pages of the open book like a pillow. She closed her eyes and put her hand to her throat, to where the knife had pressed. She hadn't known metal could feel hot and cold at the same time. Hadn't realized you could feel a sensation so long after it was gone. Hadn't expected not to be afraid, but she wasn't. When they stood at his locker, she kept her feet in her shoes, one hand long at her side. Now she waited here, not knowing how she knew but only that he would come.

A drop of liquid spat from the sky and pinpricked Evie's forehead. She opened her eyes to see James Monroe leaning against her favorite tree. He stepped over the low, leafy branch.

Evie wondered if she should sit up or stay lying down. Before she could decide, he sat next to her, legs stretched out long.

She rolled onto her side and looked up at him. "Did you follow me?"

James Monroe dipped his head low. He drew matches from his pocket and lit a cigarette, his left hand cupped backwards against his face and his elbow jerked out in the air. He jetted smoke out one side of his mouth, then rounded his lips and mouthed rings around rings, stabbing the cigarette through each one. "No virgins," he said, then laughed and looked away.

Evie took the cigarette from his hand and inhaled the way she'd practiced with Alison, remembering to push her lips out like a starlet. She imagined the swirling gray smoke dancing inside her chest was her soul. She handed the cigarette back to James Monroe, then tilted her head to blow smoky soul swirls up to the sky. She wondered exactly what the raping would entail. First base? That was a hand up her shirt, right?

James Monroe's cuticles were ragged and spotted with small scabs, his nails oddly long and tipped with crusted half-moons of grime. He handed her a piece of folded paper: the Tammy page from her notebook. Evie unfolded the paper, then smiled. He'd filled in all the blank space with Sammies.

He exhaled his last hit, angled his hand above his shoulder and flicked the butt out into the surrounding grass.

"You idiot. Don't do that!" Evie ran to where she thought the butt landed, rifling amid the flattened tangle of grass until she found it, still burning orange. She brought it back to him. "You could burn this whole place up."

"Or down." James Monroe snatched the butt from her and held it against the back of his hand, wincing until the ember died.

Evie dropped to her knees and slapped the hand holding the butt away from his other one. The spot glowed red, the angriest moon among shadows of purple less-angry moons. A burn mark like a chicken foot on the back of his hand.

It made her sick. Sad. She wanted a glass of water. No. She felt like a glass of water. Cold glass outside, something else inside, filling her shape. She touched the back of his hand with her finger, careful not to disturb the raw wound. She could feel his entire body trembling, heard his legs rustling the grass, but kept her eyes down, shining softness onto the spot.

His lips brushed against her ear. "Don't move," he whispered.

Was it going to begin now?

His mouth turned up in a half-smile and his eyes shone bright. They were not just blue, they were green, too. *Verde.* "Look."

Evie looked up slowly, the water inside her glass body barely registering a ripple.

Velvet shapes gathered in the darkening glade. A pair of black eyes, then two more. A large buck and two does, softly chewing, on the way home to their nest. Inspecting Evie Moulton and James Monroe. The male stepped over the log into the clearing and dug his nose into the spot the cigarette butt had disturbed.

James Monroe breathed so softly it felt like tiny spiders invading Evie's ear.

The buck's head reared up. He snorted air through his nostrils, as though Jim's very breath, his existence, rankled. With a tail flick, the animal bounded away in a single, silent arc, landing with a rustle and thud. The does disappeared too, as though they never even existed.

A weird, muffled sound came from James Monroe's throat. He slowly toppled onto Evie's sleeping bag, crying into the plaid flannel.

Evie's face grew warm as her heart pumped blood to her chest, her cheeks, her lips. "Jimmy," she said, reaching out to touch his dirty hair. "Poor Jimmy."

TROGLODYTE

. . . . .

Sometimes I just knew things. Like when the couple in the beige station wagon dropped me off at the park, I knew it was an okay place to be. They offered to buy me a hamburger and to hang out with them before I dived into fugitive life. It was tempting, but I was impatient to see the world with my own vision. *This is my world,* I thought, running my fingers along the manicured hedge that separated Precita Park from the street. *My world,* the expanse of lush lawn. The kiddy yard at the far end, metal swing chains clanking in the breeze of invisible riders, slide rusty at the flat bottom portion where puddles had gathered and dried over the years, monkey bars with rings on a pole. *My world, my world,* till I'd studied it all and landed back where I'd begun.

Some kids had arrived and sat cross-legged, laughing, under a tree. Maybe they were runners too. I wanted to survive, so I thought I should mingle. I sat on a bench to devise an opening. *Hey. Hi. Hello.*

One of them came over and said, "Hey. I'm Spider. You new?" He was wrangly, and his left eye blinked a lot. I didn't kid myself he was flirting.

"I guess," I said. At fourteen, I felt ancient, practically medieval.

"You hungry?" Blink, blink.

Shrug, shrug, I answered, not wanting to give too much away, not
so soon.

He took me over to the tree and introduced me to The Affiliation.
"Like a singing group?" I asked, because what did I know?

"More like a family," Zeke said. He looked older than the others, with
bits of red beard coming in along the jaw.

"But mostly like an affiliation," Sky said, pulling her shimmery gold
hair into a ponytail, then letting it fall down her back. Everyone laughed
except me.

Those two were the glorious ones, real movie stars who'd lived on
the street for a while. Then there was Princess. She wasn't what I'd call
pretty, with her square thighs and tiny black eyes, but her hands were
razzle-dazzle. Curiously, no one asked me my name. Maybe it was some
kind of street etiquette.

Spider, Princess, and I went into a grocery store on the corner. While
Spider and I debated U-No versus Abba-Zaba, Princess's paws went to
work, giving a thumbs-up as she left the store alone, now pregnant under
her poncho. Shoplifting wasn't in the original blueprint of my new life,
but I was pretty hungry.

We hunkered under a tree to share berry pies, beef sticks, and Squirt.
Afterward, we watched the weather change. Summertime here made no
sense at all. The fog was unruly, shifting with the wind and the light. It
whispered and moaned—or was that Zeke and Sky on the other side of
the tree?—and slid down like poured velvet over the low rooftops. Fog
didn't make my head hurt like the dark clouds at home did; for that I
was overjoyed. Those were miserable days, when the sky hammocked
over my head, and all I could think were cheesy thoughts. Poor me, blah-
biddy blah. I was still glad I'd left, so what if the chill burned through my

thin T-shirt and my teeth were clacking to beat the band. Princess took pity, pulled her infamous poncho over her head, and sent it my way. It was scratchy and smelled vaguely of dog, but hers was a gleaming gesture anyhow.

When I flipped it right side out and saw the big butterfly crocheted right into the fabric, I about flew up to heaven. Last year, in Science, I kept a caterpillar in a jam jar next to my bed. The creature went ravenous, eating for days, till it fell sleep and became what's called a chrysalis, though it looked more like a turd. My brother and I watched it, waiting, with him always badgering and pressing against me, honking my new boobs when no one was looking. When the chrysalis cracked open and out burst this insect of paradise, I was so surprised my pencil went bang into my brother's eye. He'd worn glasses since he was an infant, so it wasn't like he was going to be an expert in the world of microscopes or binoculars. I said I was sorry a gazillion times, but you can't beg forgiveness from a belt. I took the butterfly outside so it could live in its world. As I watched it flit from our fence to the bricks, then beyond, I knew it was time to quit being a turd and hitchhike my way out of there.

They sat on a bench wearing matching fuzzy, white tam-o'-shanters. The mother cracked open a newspaper. The daughter scampered into the sandbox. They were like Scottie dog magnets. Watching them made my heart ache, but there was a happy side to the ache, like when Spider asked if I was new.

I waved, to ingratiate my winning ways. The mother settled in reading the paper, but the daughter waved back with both arms, which was surprising, me being a stranger.

"Score!" Princess called, waving a tuna sandwich, one hand still in the trash can. She tore it into fours and handed a section to each member of The Affiliation.

Spider's left eye blinked. He tore his quarter in half and handed a piece to me, keeping the crusty old corner for himself.

"Oh, I'm sorry!" Princess said, then started sexy-dancing to music only she could hear.

"Who were you waving at?" Spider asked me.

"No one." I felt selfish: here he was giving me part of his sandwich, and I didn't want to share in return.

"Time to cruise," Zeke announced, tucking his shirt in his pants. Sky was brushing her glorious hair. They were done making out. "We do afternoons at Dolores."

"Who's she?" The name sounded sad, but I was instantly jealous.

"Dolores Park, man. You'll dig it." Zeke kissed Sky's cheek.

I wasn't ready to be tied down to feeling like a fifth wheel in couple world. "You go ahead. I'll see you later, okay?"

"Don't lose my poncho." Princess waggled a schoolteacher finger at me. "We'll need it for breakfast."

It was new to want something and get it. And it wasn't like me to go and sit on a bench next to strangers. I blame the butterfly poncho.

The mother glanced up, crossed her legs, turned a page. I sat quietly, developing a crush on the mother's straw basket. It had flowers woven around the handle and an exotic, farm girl air. I watched the kid have a love affair with the slide. Up and down, up and down. Both hands in the air, a loud, husky "whee!" on the way down, and a mother with one eye on guard: danger and safety were an enchanting couple. Suddenly, the wind gusted and barked.

Sheets of the mother's newsprint rose up from the bench and soared over the sandbox, snapping and crackling like large, gray gulls. The kid shrieked from the slide, stretching out her arms. The mother and I jumped from the bench, chasing and snatching at the paper. But the wind kept laughing and teasing, puffing them just out of reach. The kid slid down to help us, and we were breathless and hysterical by the time the wind quit and we retrieved all the pieces. I tried to flatten out the ones I'd caught, but they were pretty much ruined.

"Don't bother," the mother said. "No good news today, and tomorrow there'll just be more of it." Her eyes were the color of the fog. She had brown, curly hair like Annette Funicello. "Thanks anyway."

"My pleasure," I said. I think I curtsied.

"Let's play," the kid said, and pulled on my hands. Her voice was deep and croaky, not the high-pitched kind most little things have. She looked just like the mom, only smaller. We amused ourselves with "Oh Mary Mack All Dressed in Black With Silver Buttons All Down Her Back" while the mother performed surgery on an orange she produced from the basket. She placed a cloth napkin on her lap, worked off the peel in a spiral, then removed the veiny threads. Even picked out the individual seeds. I myself don't mind seeds; if you make a funnel with your tongue, they spit far. But I was not about to quibble. When she reached over, pressed a section of orange into my palm, and said, "I'm Linda and that's my daughter, Summer," the fog cracked open, and a warm breath of sunshine poured down.

The Affiliation returned shortly after dark. They had scored some green off an old dude outside the church and splurged on burritos, even brought one back for me. "You're our good luck charm," Sky said.

"But I wasn't even there," I said, biting into beans and rice.

"Which makes your magic even more profound." Zeke pulled at his sparse chin hairs like a professor.

Sky wedged a candle nub into an empty soda can and lit it. "For ambiance," she said, with a French accent.

"Just like camping," Spider said.

"Yeah, right," said Princess.

We sang the choruses from Top Twenty songs until the candle went out then spooned like kittens under a blanket that Spider pulled out from a hiding place in a hedge, the lawn cold and soft on our faces. The city sounded gentle at night. The whoosh of tires on damp pavement, an occasional honk. I slept with my hands jammed in the front pockets of my jeans, safeguarding my section of orange.

■ ■ ■ ■ ■

At dawn, our tree filled with the chatter of gossipy birds. My side ached where I'd rolled onto a root, but I kept my mouth shut. Spider and Zeke had disappeared. Sky whispered and whined to her dreams. Princess was buried under a curtain of brown hair; it didn't look like she was breathing at all. I tucked my chin in my hands and observed the morning world come to life. Dads stood on street corners with lunch boxes and thermoses. Busses chuffed and groaned. Kids in uniforms with white socks and oxfords carried books, looking both ways.

My hair was stinky and so was I. I needed a bath, though a shower would be okay too. I've never understood standing up to wash if you have the chance to do it sitting or lying down. My father said baths were for people who like to sit around in their own filth. I guess I didn't mind contemplating the world in my own filth, although I preferred to contemplate daily.

The boys returned with donuts and Styrofoam cups of hot choco-late. "Mmm, breakfast in bed," I said. "Thanks, Spider."

He patted me on the head and said, "Hey, no prob, chickie." His blink was starting to get to me.

As it turned out, Princess wasn't dead at all. Her head popped up, and she shot me a look like, *Don't be too nice to my man.* I peeked at Spider, but he was engrossed in a jelly donut.

The Affiliation invited me to come along to Dolores, but again, I declined. I returned to the kiddy yard. Yesterday's newspapers were still in the trash, so I dug up a piece and entertained myself with society news. Ladies with big teeth and tall hairdos like furry Russian hats smiled and dangled their sparkly earrings at men in white shirts and dark ties. It seemed glamorous to have a roman numeral after your name. I'd like to have a V after mine, like a peace sign. I was imagining my hair piled high when Summer ran up and tugged on my hand, jabbering in that surpris-ing voice for me to play "Oh Mary Mack."

"Summer, shame on you," Linda said. "You can't treat people like that." She sat on our bench and set the flowered basket at her feet.

I decided my good deed for the day would be to broaden Summer's horizons. "Hey, no prob, chickie," I said, and led Summer into the sand-box, my platinum bouffant sparkling in the fog, my diamond earrings irradiating a laser beam light show. She made that pouty *You've got to be kidding; why are you ruining my perfect world?* face that kids sometimes make when you point them in a direction they're not used to, but in a short time she was flying, screaming for me to push harder. Once we worked out the kinks, she was a natural, and I only had to push every other time to keep her at maximum height.

This time, Linda had two oranges in her basket. She taught me how to peel away the skin in a spiral and hold it just so, letting it drop lightly into itself to create the illusion of a perfect orange globe.

On their way home, Linda and Summer stopped at the grocery store Princess had kyped from. I strolled parallel to them in the park, weighing the naked orange in my hands under the poncho. Linda came out with a brown bag. Summer gnawed on a meat stick. I panged for that meat stick so badly, I allowed myself a section of orange. They turned the corner on a street called Treat. Treat V could be a good last name.

I shaded my eyes from the glare of the fog, following a safe distance behind. Treat was a dead-end street. At the top a hillside of grass—an ocean of it!—waved hello. Linda and Summer went into a small cottage with brown shingles, white window frames, and a front yard tall with sour grass and onion grass and lemon grass and all other kinds of wild grasses I suddenly remembered chewing when I was younger, in the eighth grade. The lights inside turned on, warm with electricity, like a bonfire in a forest. I sat on the curb with my orange. When the street-lights blinked on, I allowed myself another section, funneled my tongue, and spit out the seeds. I was shaky when I slunk into the yard, but the stink of my hair pushed me on. I listened with mouse ears for danger or clues, but all I heard was the far-off yipping of Chihuahuas.

Three dark, dirty windows sat at ground level, below the rest of the house. I popped in another section of orange and wormed around the side opposite the front door. I beat back a blanket of spider web and pushed aside a bush blooming stickers and balls of spitbug spit. At the bottom of some stairs was a small green door with a window. It was unlocked, so I stepped inside and closed the door behind me. I stood there, like an alley cat, waiting for the shape of the room to appear, enjoying the swampy basement air and the orange on my tongue, listening to Linda's and Summer's footsteps on their floor, my ceiling. I was well-versed in the ways of the dark, having spent many open-eyed nights in bed, practicing looking into it and finding things I had lost. My favorite No. 2 pencil? I found it at the back of my lucky charm shoe box by thinking about it when I couldn't go to sleep. Ditto my blue and yellow argyle sock, at the bottom of my brother's bed. I had always marveled at the size of darkness, how you could either feel completely closed in by it, like you were wrapped in black wool, or it could stick you smack in the middle of the universe, like you were a sun or an exploding star. Once my eyes got the hang of things, I could make out a pile of books on the floor. And a sleeping bag. As though they were waiting for me.

■ ■ ■ ■ ■

A clock radio buzzed in the morning. A bedroom was directly over my head. Loud music came on. There was thunder up there, like war drums or jungle boogie, followed by footsteps. They were dancing. I wanted to get up and dance too, but once I latched onto the hot smell of bacon and eggs and slightly burned toast, I fell under its spell. I rolled over and pressed my face into the poncho I'd made into a pillow, and smashed my fist into my gut to quell the pangs. To distract myself, I memorized their basement, my new world. No car, which was good: no one would be coming here anytime soon. One wall was lined with old newspapers, tied and stacked up to the ceiling. Stuffing exploded from the arm of a red leather chair next to a tall bookcase crammed with books. *Ivanhoe.*

Pollyanna. A familiar, throaty caterwaul came from above. Then Linda's exasperated voice: ",,,starving children in India." Back home, I ruled in Paralyze Tag and was able to stay frozen a long time. I waited until the front door closed, the key turned in the lock, and their footsteps grew faint as they walked down Treat. They thoughtfully left the bathroom window open and positioned the dirty clothes hamper just below it.

First thing I did was use the toilet. I'd been holding it, and the pain was enormous. The bathroom was tiled in pink and green. It was comfortable, the way bathrooms are. Even though I was alone, I lit some matches to burn off the stink, then set out to explore. The cottage was tiny, as though made by elves, with paneled walls and dotted lace curtains. The kitchen had a restaurant-style booth and a counter that opened into the living room with a real fireplace. There was only one bedroom; Summer's portion of it was sectioned off with a screen and had a rainbow and pink fluffy clouds painted right on the wall.

Back home, our furniture was cheap and plastic and new. Here, the coffee table was antique, posed on curvy legs and dotted with cigarette burns. An armchair had teeth marks around one of its ankles. The big bed had a buttoned-leather headboard, scratched and marked. A Chinese-style black lacquer jewel box flourished necklaces and bracelets. The closet was bursting with dresses that smelled of oranges; I pictured Linda's foggy eyes as I pressed my face against a bouquet of sleeves. Summer's bright play clothes smelled fresh, like nature and animals. Or was that me?

The pipes shrieked when I turned off the faucet. I slid into the water and watched myself turn pink. I felt more naked than usual, as though my skin were brand-new. My scar felt gorgeous under water, and I played

"Chopsticks" on it, which helped me relax. My first assignment was to pick a new name and try it on for size.

Autumn Treat V was much too sophisticated to pretend to be shipwrecked at sea or to mastermind hand races, right versus left, like she did in the tub when she was young. She was too glamorous to play farting submarines or to splash "The Star-Spangled Banner" with her thumbs. Autumn Treat V was the loneliest water nymph ever. She plunged under the sea to a bubble-filled underwater world, gliding through kelp, cavorting with seahorses. It was so sad and beautiful she wanted to cry. When Autumn Treat V discovered it was impossible to cry under water, I decided Autumn wasn't a good name after all, and it was time to get out of the tub.

The softness of the towels made me twinge with hunger. I tucked one around me, admiring the hush, scheming on bacon and eggs. When it came to kitchen messes, I knew what was what, having slaved hours and often over a hot Shake & Bake. I was the champ of peanut butter and apple sandwiches, and heating up pork and beans and brown bread from the can. I didn't mean to be a glutton, but before I knew it, I'd fried up five pieces of bacon and scrambled the two eggs they left me. I ate like royalty—one bite of egg to two bites of bacon and no interruptions from the peasants at all—and grew fat and full. I found a washing machine in a little backyard hutch and put my dirty clothes in it, then decided to put my best foot forward. Naked as a lark under my towel, I cleaned up the kitchen, washing all the plates and bowls and cups and glasses and the big greasy pan—even theirs, which was no small thing considering how much I hate to wash dishes, and everyone knows it ages your hands before their time—and stacking them neatly on the counter.

I put my clothes in the dryer and padded from room to room, opening cupboards, fingering papers. I knew this wasn't really my world, but being alone there was like suddenly having answers to everything. Inside the jewel box were gold bracelets with leopard fur, necklaces of sparkling gems, dangly bead earrings. I tried them all on, posing like the nude statues I'd pored over in art class, aiming for a Michelangelo effect that didn't pan out. My clothes were still damp, so I found a paisley dress in the closet, one that made me look almost 16 and busty if I pulled it tight in the back and contorted my shoulders together.

I turned on the radio for ambiance. "Dear Kasey Kasem, This may seem like a strange request, but I would like to dedicate this song to my wife, Bertha. Thank you, Kasey, from Joe in Cincinnati, Ohio. And now, number eighty-one in today's Top One Hundred."

That troglodyte song came on, the one they'd been playing for the last few weeks. I sang and boogied as the guy told the story of going back to caveman time, and being tired of dancing alone and grabbing a cavewoman named Bertha Butt by the hair. At the end of the song, I flopped on the big bed and flipped off the radio. I wanted to commemorate everything: the crack in the ceiling, the sun through the curtains, the blue chiffon scarf draped over the gold-edged mirror, naked with the jewelry, groovy in the dress. If Linda took me in, I could sleep on the couch. I could wash dishes and clothes and babysit Summer, so Linda could go shopping with her friends. Fantasy buzzed in my brain like a yellow jacket, making me woozy with hope, which is why I didn't worry about the footsteps on the front walk until a metal clang rang like a gunshot at the door. My whole skin electric, I bolted to the bathroom, leaped out the window and ran all the way down the hill to the park, aware of nothing but the slap of my bare feet on the sidewalk.

When I got to the tree, my throat was burning; I thought my chest would explode. My pits stank, something that had just started happening lately, which was really stupid and annoying and was probably ruining my dear Linda's dress. I pushed deep into the hedge, found The Affiliation's stash and wrapped myself in their blanket to calm down. A few minutes later I exploded again, this time in giggly relief, when the mailman strode down the hill.

I stayed blanketed in the hedge for a while, observing the comings and goings of the park. A brown Chevy van was parked at one end, music thumping from its speakers. At the kiddy yard end, Summer was gangbusters on the baby slide. Linda stood next to her in the sand, shaking out one shoe, then another, then the other again. If sand was getting in her shoes, why didn't she just step out of the box? Why wasn't she sitting at her bench? I didn't want to think my people were mental, so I crossed my fingers and practiced some telepathy until I heard screams of laughter.

The Affiliation spilled out the back of the van, heading across the park toward my people. Spider was spinning with airplaned arms. Princess lurched like a zombie. Sky stuck her foot out, and Zeke tripped over it every time he stepped forward. Every single time. When he finally hit the dirt, Sky fell on top of him, then Spider piled on top of her, and Princess on top of them all, laughing like they'd never seen anything as funny as themselves falling to the ground. They'd stop and hold their stomachs and gasp and then start all over again. Spider beat his hands on his chest like King Kong, shouting, "Monkey bars! Come on! Let's play!" and they all started hooting like chimpanzees or maybe orangutans; I could never remember which was which. But they were running toward the kiddy yard with their hands on the ground and their rumps in the air, hooting and screaming. One minute, everyone was in their own orbit, minding their business, and the next, all the planets were about to collide. My pit stink was really flaring up now.

Summer stood at the top of the baby slide and windmilled *hello* to The Affiliation. "Watch me!" she hollered, and slid down the chute as if it were a monster roller coaster. That's when I understood why Linda was there. She was standing guard over the little nut. Protecting her from The Affiliation who were galloping toward them like beasts.

At that exact, specific moment, I wished I were older. If I were fifteen, I would know how to behave when I needed to do one very small yet preposterously important thing. I let the blanket drop to the ground. "Yaaaaaaaaah," I yelled, bursting out of the bushes and heading straight for The Affiliation. My voice sounded strangulated; I was shocked by its force. It must have shocked The Affiliation too, because Princess and Sky screamed like girls and veered off in opposite directions. Zeke and Spider, who had started racing each other and were farther ahead, stopped in their tracks and loped back to check out the commotion.

They tackled me from both sides, and we hit the ground. My wind got knocked all the way out, but I didn't care. I couldn't really breathe, but I sneaked a look toward the kiddy yard. Linda and Summer were nowhere to be seen.

"Are you high?" Spider pressed his face close to mine. His Dentyne breath was spicy-sweet. "Where'd you go last night?"

My heart skipped, waiting for his blink.

"Where'd you get that dress?" Princess demanded, slapping my shoulder. "And where's my poncho?"

"Hey, brothers and sisters." Zeke was all dad business now. "Let's not freak out."

Sky nuzzled her face into Zeke's neck. "Let's go back to the van and smoke a peace pipe."

"Sure," I said. "I'll bring the poncho back tomorrow."

Princess scowled. I followed them to the brown van, though I couldn't care less about smoking a bogus peace pipe. The universe was intact. I hoped Linda hadn't recognized her dress.

Music was still blaring from inside the van when we got there, and Zeke had to knock twice on the back door—really pound it. The door opener was older, in his twenties. He wore a red knit cap and round, mirrored glasses. His black hair bushed out at the sides and a gnarly beard grazed his chest. "If this van's rockin', don't bother knockin'," Blackbeard growled, and started to pull the door closed again.

Zeke stopped the door with his hand. "Come on, man. My kids need a peace pipe."

The van's inside walls were covered in posters that glowed. I had never smoked dope before. Zeke promised it would make everything float but instead my brain closed over. The dark clouds of home rushed in like a riptide. I felt dizzy and sick. "Quick, she's going to blow!" Spider and Zeke picked me up and helped me outside. I heaved into the gutter, too tired to be embarrassed. There wasn't all that much to heave. When I woke up, it was dark. I was in the hedge, under the blanket. The Affiliation and the brown van were gone. I had to go home.

As I ran leaping from shadow to shadow, I knew it was peculiar that home meant the cottage at the top of the hill. I blame my big, pounding heart for making me slam the basement door as though it was my old bedroom door. For making me forget I was supposed to be incognito. As soon as I stepped into the dark, everything above me that was normal suddenly became very not.

"Who's there?" Linda called in a scaredy-cat voice.

I almost answered and slapped my hand over my own mouth to shut up.

"Mommy, do we have a ghost?" The reedy voice of Summer.

"Don't be silly," Linda said. "It's just a lost kitty." Then footsteps and the front door opening.

I squeezed myself behind the red chair with the popped-out stuffing and shut my eyes. I knew that didn't mean I was invisible or anything, the way I used to think when I was young, but it made me feel better. The same way hiding in the upstairs hall closet made me feel safe. It smelled Lysol-clean in there, and before I got too big to fit, I could squeeze in behind the stack of soft towels. Close my eyes. Drift away.

The basement door opened. I held my breath, my heart pounding in my ears worse than a parade of drums. I remembered reading about the perils of Anne Frank and was sorry for her all over again.

"Here, kitty, kitty," Linda called. A flashlight beam swirled around the room. "Come out, come out, you naughty little cat."

How badly I wanted to see her, to look into Linda's brave eyes. To follow the curl of her hair. I waited a long time after she left before crawling out from my spot. I would have to be a much more careful and quiet ghost. I lay back on Sky's poncho on the old sleeping bag and smoothed my hands down the front of Linda's paisley dress, now dirty and torn. I wondered if anyone missed me, my mother with her premonitions, my father with his backhand. Or my brother, now that my boobs weren't around for the honking. No doubt he was wallowing in the glory of my absence, stuffing his face with the chocolate pudding I made before I left. If nobody missed me, then who was I? I slid a book from the shelf and blew dust off the top. The leaves were dingy and yellowed, but in back were stiff, glossy pages with black-and-white photos. Pollyanna was a teacher's pet kind of girl, with queer, waist-length ringlets and plain librarian clothes. Her smudged, dark eyes made her look old and seductive. I stayed up all night and read the whole book.

· · · · ·

The water was cold. I was climbing a white ladder that went straight from the ocean to the clouds when the creak of the front door woke me up. I struggled to stay asleep. I didn't want to lose the feeling of climbing the ladder knowing that something truly magnificent was at the top. Something better than I don't know what: unicorns or egg salad sandwiches or a sectioned-off corner of a room behind a screen painted with rainbows and clouds. But I didn't have time to figure it out. I had eaten three of those mini white-powdered donuts, fallen asleep in the tub, and now there were intruders. I snatched Linda's dress from the floor and jammed out the window.

"Put this under your tongue, and then we'll tuck you into bed," I heard Linda say. "Did you leave your dirty bathwater in the tub?"

"I didn't take a bath today." Summer's kazoo voice echoed against the tiles. My tub water glugged as it swirled down the drain. "If there's a kitten in the basement, can we keep it? Please?"

"Maybe," said Linda. "If there's a kitty."

I had never been outside with no clothes on before, and I felt like a giant baby. I was like the Pink Panther from the waist down, because I loved to make the water as hot as it would go. I waited until the toilet flushed before tiptoeing around to the laundry hutch in the back.

I buried her dress at the bottom of the pink plastic laundry basket and that's when I discovered the real bonanza. A white sweater so soft it could have been made from exotic rabbits, wafting her unique perfume. There was a small yellow stain on the front of the left thigh of white jeans. I imagined Linda drinking champagne with a prince or a baron, laughing over a private joke about snowflakes, his hand knocking her glass as he brushed tousled hair from her eyes. With safety pins at the waist and the long legs cuffed up, her jeans fit me perfectly; I felt like an angel or a cloud. I wished I had eaten more of those donuts, but I couldn't bear to leave Linda and Summer. I slipped back into the basement and listened to *The Sound of Music* with them. By the time "Edelweiss" came on, I was more than halfway back to that white ladder feeling.

There was a man in our cottage. I knew because when the sound of the doorbell woke me up, it wasn't a di*ng-dong, Avon calling* sound. The person who rang it had a heavier hand, attached to a bulkier footstep with a wider space between steps. The floor vibrated differently and so did the joists and the beams over my head; their boards creaked, not used to his weight. I heard him try to make Summer laugh. The old nickel behind the ear trick, no doubt. She wasn't having any of it. She fussed and whined and gibbered baby-talk, while Linda apologized and admonished, administrating tuna casserole. I wondered what he was doing up there, but it didn't take long to find out. Summer went to bed right after dinner. Probably still tasting raspberry Jell-O on her dark-red tongue.

I was getting so worked up and hungry thinking about tuna casserole and Jell-O that I hadn't noticed the radio music playing above me or the little shuffling steps or Linda's muffled laughter. It was the "Troglodyte" song again. Linda and the man thumped their feet wildly. A little too wildly, because I heard her call out something like "Jazz!" before the scream. Then there was a scraping sound, maybe wood against linoleum. But it could have been wood against bone or hand against backside or fist against head or shoe against shoulder. All these possibilities made me crazy, and maybe I cried, "Stop!" Or maybe I kicked the red chair, I can't really recall, but the next thing I knew, Linda and Jazz were outside my basement door window.

They were in profile by flashlight, just like those cameo ovals above the TV at my old house. I timed my roll behind the red chair while they were opening the door. The light flashed in circles, like Hollywood searchlights, but it sure didn't feel like the Academy Awards. Mostly, I tried not to think about spiders or mice or to jinx myself into sneezing from the cloud of dust my rolling kicked up.

"That sleeping bag always been there?" Jazz asked. I wanted to hate his voice but I couldn't. It was just a regular TV commercial voice, with no accent. A voice that sold things.

"I don't know," Linda answered, all girlish and concerned. "I never really poked around down here before. I don't like to go to dark places alone."

"Honey, that's just an open invitation to trouble."

An open invitation? I clamped my hand over my mouth to keep from shouting.

"Don't you worry," he went on. "We'll get rid of your ghost." The zipper pull tinkled as Jazz threw my sleeping bag over his arm. "Like you said, it's probably just a cat."

· · · · ·

I was so worried about making noise and instigating another research expedition, I hardly slept that night. I must have stayed curled in a tight ball the whole time, because when I finally woke up, my legs were still sleeping and prickly. I didn't look much like an angel or a cloud when I crawled out from behind that chair. I was starving out of my skull. I listened hard for a while to make sure the upstairs was empty, even though I knew it was far later than I'd ever slept before.

It was so peculiar when the little green door wouldn't open. I kept turning the knob this way and the other, it didn't catch and open the way it always had before. My brain refused the reality, and I kept making up possible/impossible excuses for the door not opening. It had swelled up during the night. The house had shrunk. I was still asleep, dreaming the door wouldn't open. Something was wrong with my hands.

I was a much better athlete in P.E. than evidenced by my window-breaking arm that morning. I would have broken the window perfectly if *Pollyanna* hadn't been so heavy and I wasn't so hungry. I didn't see the blood or the jagged flap of skin until I was outside. I don't know how long I stood in the front yard. I was mesmerized, hypnotized, transmogrified by the color of my blood. How could little old me—skinny and scabby, dressed in filthy clothes that weren't mine and didn't fit—be filled with such a beautiful, rich color? And the blood ran like water too. I always thought it would be more lazy, like maple syrup. It was all so amazing I wanted to cry.

But I didn't. I held my dripping arm away from me and walked to the park. I found a sheet of binder paper with a spelling test on it (I tried not to be too hard on Nancy; "renaissance" wasn't an easy word) and wrapped it around my arm, then scrounged up a brown bag with the rest of somebody's lunch inside. A bunch of grapes and half a salami sandwich, both of which I ate too fast, making my stomach ache. I tried to see what time it was by the sky, but the fog was so high and bright, I couldn't even pinpoint the sun. I tried, remembering *The Sound of Music* songs to make me feel better, but "crisp apple strudels" and "schnitzel with noodles" made me hungrier, which was the opposite of the point.

The brown van was parked in its usual place. The driver's seat was empty, but the vehicle shook on its wheels. Voices rose from the back, growing louder and more agitated. Suddenly, the rear doors banged open, and The Affiliation flew out. Spider first, his blue work shirt unbuttoned and flapping like a superhero cape in slow motion, followed by Sky, ethereal and weightless as usual, then Zeke and finally Princess, who was topless and crying. Her feet scarcely touched ground when Blackbeard hopped out, slammed the back doors, and bounded into the driver's seat. The van sped away, tires squealing. Princess's red face was twisted. Weird animal sounds came from her mouth. Her boobs were slouchy and loose. She was no longer just a girl but a woman. I wished I had her poncho so I could give it to her right now, but I felt so far away. Like I was watching them on the five o'clock news instead of the whole thing happening right in front of me.

"Come," said a voice at my elbow.

Linda was standing there, her straw basket over her arm and one hand over Summer's eyes. She grabbed my clean hand and turned me away from the scene.

I wanted to look back over my shoulder, to see Spider removing his shirt and wrapping it around Princess, blinking only for her. To see that Princess had quieted down and Sky was shushing and kissing her, smoothing her hair. But I couldn't look. Didn't glance. Didn't try. I didn't want to be disappointed. I didn't want Linda to let go.

We were walking so fast, the only thing I could concentrate on was that straw basket with the plastic flowers. It reminded me of Little Red Riding Hood, and by the time I remembered the whole story, with the grandma and Little Red and the wolf, Linda had taken me into the grocery store and marched all the way past the section where Princess kyped the Squirt and the pies, right through a curtain of beads, and into a dark storeroom. Summer waited at the doorway while Linda guided me past crates of lettuce and carrots, past shelves stacked with canned goods and sacks of flour and sugar, salt and potatoes. We went into a tiny, pale yellow bathroom lit by a bare bulb. She put down the lid and pointed for me to sit. There was nothing for me to do but obey.

She peeled away the spelling quiz, made a good lather with a rough bar of grimy soap, then carefully washed my arm. "Those are my clothes, aren't they?" she asked softly.

I couldn't bear to look down at the beautiful white pants I'd ruined with my blood, so I nodded, then stared up at the most successful no-pest strip I'd ever seen in life, thick with the bodies of flies.

"I got that sweater on sale for five dollars," she said as she swabbed my gash with alcohol. "It looks real good on you. Your skin tone is perfect for white."

She went on talking about fashion and things. I couldn't concentrate on what she was saying, but I didn't want her to stop; her voice gave me rubber tree plants in my belly. When she finished wrapping my hand in cotton, she asked me my name, and I told her.

"Well, Coco," she said. "I would be most honored if you would accept my humble invitation to dine *chez nous* with us tonight. Now, what is your favorite meal?"

It was so bizarre to find myself back in my bathtub. The white pants and the sweater had disappeared; nothing more about them was said. Linda told me to keep my messed-up hand out of the tub so the dressing wouldn't get wet; hand races were out of the question. I didn't much feel like playing farting anthems either or sea nymph. I didn't want to think or remember or plan or pretend. I just wanted to feel clean.

After I toweled off, Linda gave me a pair of blue capris and a yellow sweater. I wanted to tell her how their colors reminded me of the day when I danced in her room. The blue scarf on the mirror, the sunshine through the lace. She pointed me toward the living room with Summer, who begged for *The Sound of Music* again. Only then did I allow myself to conjecture they might let me stay. Or adopt me. I could become the nanny. Or maybe a nun.

"Coco!" Linda called from kitchen. "Time for dinner! Coco?"

I'd almost forgotten who I was.

She sat across from me in the little restaurant-style booth. I thanked her and tried to look into her fog-colored eyes but she looked away. The meat loaf was delicious, with rivers of ketchup on top and canned French-fried onions on the side. Plus au gratin potatoes with orange cheese burned just how I like. The green beans squeaked merrily against my teeth when I chewed; the pound cake with Cool Whip was heaven. Everything was so delicious, I knew leaving home was the right thing to do.

"This is my world," I told them, when Officer Kelly arrived to take me away. "This is my world."

HELP ME FIND MY KILLER

. . . . .

While making French toast and watching Geneva sit on a kitchen barstool, Peg decides two things. One, she hates pretty women, and, two, she doesn't really want to die.

Peg hates pretty women for the obvious reasons. Foremost is the fact that not even crappy sweatpants detract from Geneva's tall, thin-boned, high-cheeked, pouty-mouthed, perfect-pored watchability. The spoon dips. Her lips part. The bowl of the spoon glides vertically down a pink tongue. She nods during the swallow, swinging butter-yellow hair. Hair that Peg cut herself with a straight edge and kitchen shears one night after kiwi coolers. Hair that moves in tandem with the fringe along the bottom of Geneva's shortie T-shirt that says "Help Me Find My Killer," the words peppered by rips and tears as though stabbed by a switchblade.

Peg expertly cracks eggs into a bowl and tosses the shells over her shoulder into the compost box. She cannot unfasten her eyes from Geneva. Neither can Peg's new boyfriend Phil. Phil only *just* gave Peg permission to start calling him boyfriend after six months of grueling blow jobs, which were rewarded with half-hearted tongue jobs that lasted only half as long as Peg's BJs and left her miles from the end of the tunnel.

Peg is not jealous that Geneva reports of hour-long orgasms with what Geneva herself calls her Flavors. They are Rories or Victors or Shanes, who, after talking to her on the phone for a while (however long Geneva decides), beg her to allow them to visit. They show up in convoys of aftershave, sweets, flowers and assorted aphrodisiacs just for the privilege of attempting to whittle off her clothes and bring her to orgasm—orgasms that Geneva broadcasts through the thin-walled apartment on a regular, unabashed basis.

Peg doubts any of the Flavors have ever received BJs by merely pointing at the floor like Phil has, a sad-but-true detail of which Peg is not proud, but which she is reminded of by the burn on her knee that says *hey*. Peg is perfectly aware that as soon as she's a decade or so out of college (say, ten years and six months from now), she will be capable of accepting her body, improving her self-image, and validating her life experience. Until then she accepts that she is lucky to have what leftovers and crumbs she has, given her pretty, no, gorgeous, no, *malevolently radiant* roommate.

But then Peg remembers that pink-tongued beauty lapping at fat-free yogurt is her best friend Geneva, same as she's ever been. And Phil is the boyfriend who relieved her of her virginity and stuck around for more, *thank God*, same as he's ever been. And this is the same butter-dripping, syrup-soaked, powdered-sugar-sprinkled French-toast recipe that Peg has been following every Saturday since she first copied it down while watching cooking-show reruns on weekend mornings back in high school, waiting for Geneva to call with plans for the night. Julia Child was not a good-looking woman, but you had to respect that cleaver.

Consider this:

1) The fact that Peg loves Geneva is no secret. Peg knows it. Phil knows it. Geneva knows it. The Flavors (if they turn to see Peg watching them bestow gifts upon the goddess) know it.

2) The reason it takes Geneva the better part of a morning to lick fat-free yogurt from a spoon is because she says it creates the sound of desire at the back of her throat.

3) Geneva's doing a final paper on phone sex.

4) Now that Peg is Phil's girlfriend and he wants them to move to the next so-called level, Peg fears she may have to choose between him and Geneva. The only way she figures she can escape Geneva's spell is to kill Geneva (which would not be easy; have you ever tried to kill the person you loved most in the world?) or kill herself (which, as Peg realized earlier in the kitchen, she doesn't really want to do, given what she's certain will bear out in the next decade or so).

5) Peg is doomed.

But Peg's always been doomed. From Day One, kindergarten class, when Miss Hoagland switched Peg out from the alphabetical seating system so she would be seated next to Geneva (already exhibiting signs of temptressness with the bouncy distractions of waist-length pigtails), instead of Brian Farling, who was developing the giraffe-neck disease from trying to observe every pigtail flick and toss with the perseverance of a *National Geographic* photographer stalking the elusive orange-eyed albino she-tiger. By seating Peg next to Geneva, Miss Hoagland hoped that Peg's good manners, bland looks, and sycophantic behavior would domesticate the white tiger. Instead, Geneva's orange eyes pirated Peg away from the other children in the village and locked her in a jungle tiger's lair, where Peg, obedient captive, fell madly, dreamily, and eternally in love with her.

Thanks to alliterative surnames, Peg's deep kindergarten devotion continued uninterrupted throughout twelve years of homeroom. Peg learned Geneva's voice so thoroughly that there was not a day Geneva slept in that Peg would not call "present" in her absence. There was no homework assignment Peg would not complete, no extra-credit project she would not commandeer without insisting Geneva's name be attached; no rap, no matter how unfair the accusation, they did not share.

Peg's displays of passion and enthusiasm drew lavish rewards from Geneva. In fourth grade, when Geneva learned Brian Farling was waiting for her in the cloakroom to deliver a spectacular French kiss, Geneva told him to close his eyes, then pushed Peg in front of him. It would have been Peg's first kiss with the man she most loved had she not tripped on her shoelace and fallen onto Brian Farling, knocking him to the ground and causing him to chip a front tooth. Geneva admitted she had pushed a little hard—it was just she had so wanted Peg to get Frenched.

When all the sixth-grade girls (save Peg) were invited to Addie Hasting's birthday/slumber party, Geneva recounted all the catty details to Peg the very next day (pubic hair in the macaroni salad; Addie's drunken parents slamming doors and arguing loudly during the karaoke portion; boys, including Brian Farling, who visited for a midnight round of Spin the Bottle; names of the Confirmed Sluts). Geneva confessed she didn't even *really* have a good time without Peg there.

When Geneva announced her eighth-grade graduation party, Peg's name was first on the invitation list, with Brian Farling's second, as though that proximity might somehow implicate an attraction. This party would be swanky—not your standard Cheetos affair—with adults invited for cocktails and *hors d'oeuvres*, and semiformal attire for all. Peg arrived early to help decorate Geneva's family room with streamers and balloons and when it was done, the girls dressed together. With glitter sparkling on her shoulders and collarbones, Geneva would debut the eighth grade's first strapless dress. Peg borrowed a dress from Geneva that still bore the scent of Love's Fresh in the armpits, an aroma Peg secretly relished. Wedged tightly into Geneva's tiny pink bathroom, they brushed, rouged, glossed, and mascara'd each other. It was as though Geneva and Peg themselves were the hosting couple, and not Geneva's beautiful parents, whose gleaming tans and white teeth confirmed their elite status, something the rest of the eighth-graders and their parents took for granted.

Everyone agreed the party was the most glamorous the eighth grade had ever attended. Geneva and Peg spent most of the evening holding hands and gulping down the adults' abandoned cocktails. Flush from mai tais and perspiring from hysterics, Peg became dizzy in the limbo crush and sat on the porch to catch her breath. By the time her cheeks regained their normal sallow complexion, Geneva's glittering shoulders were nowhere to be found. Peg lurched down the hallway, where she found Geneva in the master bedroom with Brian Farling, who was dry-humping her in the pile of purses and shawls.

Peg shut the door. It was the first time she felt like she wanted to die. She shuffled back to the kitchen, where Geneva's beautiful father, who was dumping ashtrays into a large plastic sack, asked if she was feeling okay. Peg nodded, tears streaming down her face. He took Peg's hand and petted it (strangely, as though it were a cat), then bent down, suggesting a nice glass of ice water.

Peg had never seen Geneva's father's face this close. She marveled at the even spacing of his large pores, the combed wheat fields of his eyebrows with the wind all blowing in one beautiful direction. Most incredible was that he had Geneva's eyes and mouth. Peg could see that same beauty in him, and she was drunk or stupid enough to think that if only she reached out for it, perhaps, she, too, would somehow be made beautiful. She liked the way he petted her hand; it made her feel pretty and safe.

With the sounds of the limbo far away, still crying, she moved her hand, with his still around it, to her breast. The other hand she placed on his zipper. Wobbly as she was, she could see he was practically crying, too, as though he'd rather be doing anything than this. It was the second time she felt like she wanted to die, as much for what was happening to her as for what she imagined must be happening to Geneva.

They were still like that, all statues and cactus, when Geneva's mother walked in. Her lipsticked mouth was open from laughing, and she had a silver ice canister slung over her arm like a purse. She froze like a mannequin for a beautiful second, then slapped her husband and pulled Peg away. Peg felt the absence of his warmth immediately and thought about dying once again.

When Geneva's mother hissed in Peg's ear, "This never happened," Peg had already decided it never had.

Geneva's mother had more to say. "Don't tell anyone. Ever."

Peg thought she never ever would. She nodded that promise, and their reflections wobbled in the bucket.

When Peg thought about it later that night, and many nights after that, she sometimes wondered if it really had happened. She wondered if she hadn't fantasized it while imagining what it felt like to be dry-humping Brian Farling. She wondered if the hardness she felt beneath the zipper was—perhaps, in reality—just a buckle.

Peg never breathed a word to Geneva. Not when Geneva's father moved away that summer, not when Brian Farling wrote "Geneva is 1 Good Slut" across the boys'-room lockers, not when Geneva cried in Peg's lap. Not even when Geneva became cavalier with her body and started tying up her T-shirt to bare her midriff, jutting herself into the faces of grocery clerks, and taking rides in high-school boys' cars while enjoining Peg to meet her at the multiplex at midnight to tell her the movie plots so Geneva could relay them to her mother.

If Peg felt guilty later for the blossoming of Geneva's rampant promiscuity, she didn't feel guilty about it then. (And why should she?) All she remembered was the exquisite excitement of Geneva retelling her sexual safaris... how awkward, how big, how dangerous, how small.

When it came time for college, Geneva's father generously evicted a long-time nonpaying family from the small two-bedroom in the complex he owned near the university, so that Geneva and Peg could be roommates. Geneva threw her arms around Peg and jumped up and down, sending pangs of heat down the backs of Peg's thighs. They painted and decorated like newlyweds and, when the place was done, threw a small dinner party for themselves. Over candles and pot pies and a box of wine, the girls became properly soused. At midnight, Geneva announced she had a surprise, at which point she opened the door on two boys, who had been lounging in the hallway, drinking beers. Geneva turned up the soft rock, removed her top and danced—she was a natural, born for the limelight—then proceeded to seduce one of the boys. Under Geneva's supervision and watchful eye, Peg surrendered her virginity to the other, who happened to be her future boyfriend, Phil. There was just enough liquor in Peg so that she didn't have to wonder for the fourth time what it would be like to die; instead, she endured his fumblings and beer breath, and was so bold as to try to feel pleasure. The boys left the minute Geneva told them to, and the girls stayed up till it was time for Peg to make French toast. While Peg stirred sugar, salt and milk into the egg mixture, Geneva suggested ways to bring herself to orgasm. It was incredible how many times Peg brought herself to orgasm while imagining Geneva implementing those very suggestions.

Peg's outstanding stenography skills quickly landed her a job at the local police department, typing petty criminal cases on multicolored forms. Geneva despised work, and was frequently hired and fired from the many retail stores and restaurants that crowded the small but busy downtown area. Phil returned to visit the girls often, joining them for dinner, homework sessions, and, soon thereafter, for late-night escapades with Peg.

One night, the three of them were celebrating Geneva getting fired from yet another job (she was caught spreading layer-cake frosting on a customer's crotch in the walk-in). Over a coffee mug of gin, Geneva described how she pretended not to hear her boss's hand on the doorknob. Knowing he was there sparked her desire to perform, so she took off her shirt and began icing her breasts. When she ran out of frosting, her boss burst into the refrigerator, and grabbed the empty can and pastry bag, and then just stood there, slack-jawed, unable to tear away his eyes. Geneva said just describing the episode turned her on, and Phil agreed. That's when one of them got the brilliant phone-sex idea (probably Peg), and one of them decided it should be Geneva's final paper (probably Geneva). It may have been the other way around, but it was difficult to say for certain; when they got excited, the lines between them blurred.

Peg wrote this for Geneva to read:

As an infant, I suckled one of my mother's breasts while twirling a fat clammy finger around the nipple of the other. I watched two dogs hump frantically before my father rushed into the street to turn the hose on them. Once, at swimming lessons, I watched Brian Farling piss a soaring arc into the baby pool, and Mrs. Farling, who had gone Oriental for the day and outlined her eyelids with black lines like crow's wings, wore a sarong-type embroidered red dress, carried a matching fan, and smacked his wiener with the fan in front of everyone in the bleachers. The image recurred each Bratwurst Thursday in the cafeteria. When I finally made out with Brian in the cloakroom, it was awful, but the combination of live Brian plus the pool-party image in my mind nearly made me swoon. I leafed through the flesh-toned pages of my father's Playboys in the hall closet, causing me to be haunted by tweed and the smell of tennis shoes. When I first encountered the rust-and-bread smell of my period, I gazed at my newly developing body for the first time in a room lit by candles and incense. I chose lip gloss to complement my vulva (Pretty in Pink). I stood on a crowded bus on the way to a volunteer job at the hospital, hanging onto a sweaty pole while men pressed their belt buckles into my lower back. I took sips from all the adults' drinks at a party, and then went into the pantry with my friend's father and rubbed my hand along the zipper of his Dockers while he felt my bare breast with his eyes closed.

Hearing those words from Geneva's mouth was hotter than anything Peg had experienced with Phil, whose newest M.O. seemed to be "Slapping gets Peg to the end of the tunnel faster."

"What do you think?" Peg asked, sitting on her hands to hide the trembling. She waited for Geneva to ask about her father. Peg needed to talk about his eyebrows and the ice bucket.

Geneva was quiet, and her usually pretty face looked different. Kind of ugly.

Peg blinked to make sure she wasn't blind drunk, or simply wishing it were so. When she opened her eyes, Geneva was beautiful again.

"It's weird, and it doesn't make any sense," Geneva said.

"That's for sure," Phil agreed.

"It's like telling secrets, though," Geneva said.

"I bet your professor would love the idea," Peg said, clinching it.

Geneva's professor loved the idea, of course, and thought it would be great if she made recordings of all the calls and brought them in for them to listen to together on Friday afternoons. Geneva was so excited at the prospect ("Easy A!" she crowed), she didn't even bother to get a 900 number; the last thing she wanted was for her voice to be anonymous. Within a few months, the weird little speech that didn't make any sense became notorious in the university region. It was deconstructed, demonized, and analyzed in various campus newspapers, with letters to the editors, rebuttals, and scandals ensuing. Geneva became more famous than ever.

All it did for Peg was ensure that their phone rang off the hook. Day and night. Night and day. Peg took her name off the phone bill and got a cell phone, which only rang when Phil called. "Re-Phil," he'd say. "Get it?" And Peg knew.

After reliving the story of her doom all the way to the present tense, Peg returns to being Julia Child—whisking egg whites in a blue bowl, slapping soaked bread onto a hot griddle, watching Phil watch Geneva—when, suddenly, she feels it. Humiliation that in one way nauseates her and, in another, excites her. She shifts her hip and watches the air as it shimmers around the yogurt, the spoon, around Geneva's mouth saying Peg's words. *I took sips from all the adults' drinks at a party, and then went into the pantry with my friend's father and rubbed my hand along the zipper of his Dockers while he felt my bare breast with his eyes closed.*

Peg serves Phil his French toast, then watches him watch Geneva some more. She wonders what it is like to be the object of constant fantasy and speculation. She doesn't believe she wants to sleep with Geneva. She isn't even certain she knows what two women do together. Peg's jaw aches slightly from Last Night's BJ. and she waggles her chin until there is an audible pop. Last Night became worthy of capital letters when Peg asked Phil if, after all this time, she could be his girlfriend, and he said, "Sure. We should probably even take it to the next level."

"The next level?" Peg asked.

"When am I moving in?"

Phil was not Peg's end-all/be-all guy. She was not really in love with him. He was not even a very good boyfriend, what with his lust for Geneva practically a fourth person in the room whenever the three of them were together. But he was the solid green light of an EXIT sign. A step forward. A glass of water to someone dying of thirst. A breeze blowing in the other direction. Peg said she'd have to think about it.

Now Peg tries to imagine the three of them in the small apartment together, Geneva looking beautiful all the time, Phil being there all the time, Peg in the burning fires of hell. Phil lived in a dorm, so moving in with him was out. And Geneva wasn't going anywhere—it was her dad's apartment.

"That was great, babe," Phil says, pushing away his empty plate.

"Thanks." Peg takes the plate and turns, as is her habit, to wash it. Smears of strawberry syrup and mint leaves have created a Rorschach design that Peg stares at so long, the water turns cold. The syrup is Geneva. The green leaves are Peg. They are on opposite sides of the plate. It is then Peg realizes that what she's considered love—dry-humping on a pile of coats, the proximity of a boy's name, a hand on a zipper, sex tips—is not love at all. Not for Peg.

Peg turns off the water. Those muslin curtains on the window over the sink with the little butterflies: Geneva and Peg popped popcorn together and sewed them. The aqua trim around the cupboards that matches the pull-thingies: the girls had wrapped their hair in red and blue handkerchiefs while they painted them. "You're a Crip, but you'll always be my Blood," Geneva joked and daubed paint on Peg's nose. Was that love?

Not for Geneva.

Peg thought love could free her, unloose her from the self she was born with and turn her into something beautiful, with wings. She was wrong. Love couldn't do that. Not love as she knew it.

But death could.

Peg wonders, for the first time in a long time, what it is like to die. Will there really be a golden beam to scoop her up, hold her to the light like a china plate, and determine that in her next life she should come back as some kind of beauty, a sleek animal with spectacular architecture and muscular haunches?

Peg must come clean. If she is going to be with Phil—and she has to be with Phil, the pain of loving Geneva is too great—she must free herself from Geneva's unholy bonds. On the counter next to the powdered sugar is a box of RatGone, a holdover from the previous tenants. Suppose Peg were to offer Geneva some French toast? If Geneva accepted, Peg could dust rat poison onto Geneva's plate. How natural for Geneva to hang up the phone from her client, toss her yogurt into the trash, dig into the French toast, leave the soiled plate on the counter, and exit without saying a word.

Geneva hangs up the phone. She turns to Phil and Peg, yawns with an extravagant stretch, then twirls in the center of the floor, just so they both can admire all of her. "I'm going back to bed," she says, taking her yogurt with her. The offer remains unproposed, the poison undusted.

When all traces of Geneva finally evaporate, Phil scratches the pale hair beneath his bellybutton suggestively. "What's the haps for today? Back to bed? Catch a vid?"

With a fresh plan in her head, Peg says, "I have to go to the library." It is a lie and it feels good.

"Okay. See ya." Phil kisses her cheek and heads toward the door. The difference in the kiss is palpable, proprietary, and it makes the burn on Peg's knees disappear. It's definitely worth it.

When Phil is gone, Peg slaps another pat of butter on a hot skillet. Its sizzle is as exciting as that green EXIT sign, its smell as delicious as the end of that tunnel. "Gen?" she calls out, a shiver flashing up her spine. "I'm making your favorite."

Peg arranges the plate with all the necessary parts, adds a strawberry garnish just because, and takes it to Geneva.

"God, I drank too fucking much last night," Geneva says as she explodes out of the bathroom and bounces onto her bed. "French toast?" she squeals. "Gimme!" Arms outstretched, fingers dancing.

Peg watches her eat (Geneva can really pack it away, even with a hangover!), then takes the plate back to the kitchen and scours it immediately. She washes the rest of the dishes, then polishes the faucet, clears the countertops, sweeps the floor and wipes down the legs of the chairs and the stool. There is nothing left to clean. She tiptoes down the hallway and peers into Geneva's room.

Geneva is asleep on her bed, bathed in light that slants through the open bathroom door. Her chest rises and falls, but Peg presses her ear against the words "Help Me Find My Killer" anyway. Geneva's heart stutters faintly.

Peg opens the top drawer of Geneva's bureau and runs her hand through a tangle of soft, slippery things connected by satin and lace. She finds the tiny pistol with a carved ivory handle—"a little protection for my girls," Geneva's father called it—and sets it on the bureau among Geneva's hairbrushes, perfumes, and tubes.

Peg unbuttons Phil's flannel shirt and steps out of her jeans, flings her cotton panties aside. A delicate strip of lace squeaks as she pulls a pearl-studded thong up over her thighs. She leaves the bra unhooked. Geneva mumbles incoherently as Peg lies down next to her and stares at the two of them in the mirror.

There are things Peg knows about Geneva that the Casanovas and Flavors will never know. The natural color of her hair. That her middle initial stands for Elizabeth, a grandmother on her paternal side, not Eloise, as she claims. She knows the shape of Geneva's mouth when she sleeps. She knows her body odor in all its guises: the French-onion-soup smell after the dentist, the fresh-grass-and-dirt smell on her T-shirt after a bike ride, the powder-and-linen smell come morning. Peg knows Geneva likes mayonnaise on French fries, girls with answers, professors with flexible office hours. She knows Geneva gets her period three days before Peg, that Geneva's period makes her horny, that fucking gives her cramps, that Flavors ease the pain. Sometimes Geneva cries when she comes, and if she does, that Flavor is history. Geneva thinks love is a waste of time.

Peg knows all this because she is Geneva's tea bag, her chewing gum, her kleenex, her eraser, her lickspittle, her nail file. She is fallen eyelashes and red grooves on thighs from elastic. That's why Geneva needs her.

Peg wonders how she could love Geneva so much and yet still want to kill her. She feels Geneva's cool flesh next to her, imagines Geneva dead, and knows she will cry real tears over Geneva's beautiful corpse, and that her life will mean next to nothing without Geneva in it.

Peg closes her eyes and enters the long dark tunnel.

The doorbell rings. Geneva stirs slightly. Peg slips into Geneva's silky kimono and looks through the peephole. It's a Saturday-night Flavor.

She opens the door and he walks in, chocolate cherries in hand. He seems surprised to see her behind the door. "Oh. Hey. Who are you?"

She has opened this door for him maybe ten times before, and introduced herself each time. She knows his name is Rory, but he doesn't deserve it right now.

"Geneva's sister," she says.

"I see the resemblance. Is Geneva here?"

"No." Peg stretches her arms provocatively, thrusting up her breasts in Geneva's bra for him to admire. "Just me."

"What's your name?" he asks, his voice turning husky.

"What do you want it to be?" she says. This is getting interesting. She could have Ror—she stops—*a Flavor* right outside Geneva's bedroom door.

But just then, Geneva's phone rings. Peg runs into the kitchen. "Yes," she answers, with the voice she has imitated for years.

"Geneva?" It's Phil. "Talk to me."

Her heart frogs under the kimono. Why is Phil calling Geneva?

The Flavor has followed her into the kitchen. He stands in the doorway, ripping the cellophane from the chocolates, his belt buckle winking. Peg perches on Geneva's barstool and remains silent as he opens the box and pushes a candy between her lips. She lets the cherry syrup collect under her tongue before speaking to create the sound of desire at the back of her throat. She had been practicing for this moment her entire life. *"As an infant, I suckled one of my mother's breasts while twirling a fat clammy finger around the nipple of the other. I watched two dogs hump frantically before my father rushed into the street to turn the hose on them."*

The Flavor looks startled—he knows this voice well. He sets the chocolates in Peg's lap, and slips both hands under her kimono, cupping the soft satin of Geneva's bra. Peg's head is spinning inside, and she imagines this is what it's like to die, just a little.

"Once, at swimming lessons, I watched Brian Farling piss a soaring arc..."

The Flavor's eyes are really blue.

Phil hesitates, then lets out his breath. "Gimme something different, G. All I'm getting are lousy blow jobs. Six months you think she'd finally get it right."

Peg sucks in her breath. Bastard.

"I'm getting head right now," she says, and she doesn't care if it is her own voice. Why should she care, with the Flavor down on his knees in front of her and she didn't even have to point to the floor. She would have liked to. "Don't you want to come over and watch?" She pops in another chocolate; they make her brave and delicious.

"Geneva? Is that you?"

Peg feels a new kind of thrill when she hears the break in his voice. She runs her hand through the Flavor's hair and then tugs it. She likes the way his head snaps back. "Of course it's me. Who did you think it was?" She is Geneva again. Damn, she is so good at this!

"Are you really getting head right now?"

"Phil, I'm having so much fucking fun right now I'm gonna give you this for free." Peg thinks of Brian Farling as she records a big fat zero in Geneva's account book, sets the timer for three minutes, and describes everything to Phil. About Geneva sick from RatGone, the gun on the bureau, and the pearl-studded thong that the Flavor is pulling down around her ankles. She tells him about the Flavor's tongue moving toward her thighs. Tells him about her hand on the Flavor's head and how she can smell chocolate-cherry liqueur on their breath. She tells him about her foot pressed high up on the refrigerator and wanting to kill Geneva so that she and Phil can be together.

By that time, Phil's breath is ragged in her ear in the way that only happens when he's about to come hard *and* slap her. She hangs up so she doesn't have to hear it. The Flavor looks up at her with glazed eyes, his hand working between his legs, belt buckle clanking at his thigh. He hasn't heard a thing she's said.

The phone rings again. "I'm coming over," Phil says.

Peg's pushing the Flavor out the door when Geneva calls her name.

Geneva is gray and sweating; the room smells rank. "I don't feel well," she says.

Peg snatches a gym duffel to the side of the bed and Geneva throws up into it. Geneva curls into a fetal position, teeth clenched, arms wrapped around her flat tummy, shivering with fever. She's even prettier when she's sick. Peg rubs her back and murmurs her name.

"What happened?" Geneva asks.

Peg is the superhero of superliars, Florence Nightingale of the damned. "I was washing dishes and noticed that somebody left the

RatGone up on the counter next to the powdered sugar. You must have put it in your coffee this morning or something." Lying to her like this makes Peg even hotter. Oh yes, this is love. She can feel it. "I called Poison Control and they talked me through it. I kind of saved your life."

"Omigod, thank you," Geneva says, overcome by waves of recuperation and gratitude. She is sobbing and kissing Peg's hands, her feet, her breasts. "I just want you to know before I die that I will dedicate my life to you. Whatever you want, whatever you need . . . "

Peg hears Phil's keys jangling at the front door.

Phil runs into Geneva's room and sees Peg sitting on her bed, in her underwear, with Geneva in her shortie T-shirt, fevered, and wrapped around Peg.

"Don't let that dirty slut touch you! I love you and I want to marry you." Phil pulls Geneva from Peg; her clawed hands rake at Peg's skin. "I want to take you away from all this," he says, covering Peg's neck in kisses. "To our own private island, where I'll treat you like a queen, and we won't tell Geneva, we won't even let her come visit."

But Geneva wants everything, she always has, even things she doesn't give a shit about. Geneva grabs her pistol from the bureau and bam! shoots it into Phil's stomach, then crawls to Peg and clasps her in her arms.

No. It's Phil who grabs the gun and shoots Geneva once, twice, a hundred times. Peg covers her head to ward off the gore, and when it's over, Phil takes her gently into his arms, and kisses her. Peg shivers with horror and delight, watching Geneva's breath bubble in blood. She comes very, very close to the end of the tunnel.

No, that's not it either. It's still Phil who grabs the gun, but it's not Geneva he shoots, it's Peg. Peg he mercifully shoots straight in the heart, Peg who is ignored and left to die, looking for the golden beam behind the muslin butterflies, watching Geneva and Phil fold their beautiful and awful selves together like dirty sheets.

That's it, Peg thinks, as she looks at herself, having blown through the end of the tunnel. Her cheeks are rosy and the too-small bra has slipped around her elbows like a harness. Stray pearls from the ripped thong dig into her thighs. There is a way out. Of course there is. All Peg needs is a vision.

CALL IT A HAT

. . . . .

Dmitri Shostakovich—Concerto in C minor for Piano, Trumpet, and Strings, Op. 35. *Orchestration: solo piano, solo trumpet, and strings.*

Igor Stravinsky—The Rite of Spring. *Orchestration: piccolo, 3 flutes, alto flute, 4 oboes, English horn, 3 clarinets, E-flat clarinet, bass clarinet, 4 bassoons...*

Lydia tried to concentrate on the program notes, but couldn't keep from glancing at her wristwatch. Three minutes past eight. The orchestra was seated, the instruments tuned, the conductor had yet to appear. Ushers continued seating latecomers. Lydia's neck dampened the collar of her special-occasion blouse. She fought the urge to recross her legs, and forced herself to remain still. Just a bit longer, and second-row, center was hers for the night.

In the concerto for piano, trumpet, and strings, Shostakovich combines humor and introspection side by side. Sudden shifts from one temperament to another juxtapose the naïve with the complex, and humor with sorrow.

"Excuse me," a gentleman tapped her knee. "I believe you're in my seat."

"I am?" she drawled softly, feigning surprise. It was acceptable practice at the symphony for cheap-seaters to migrate forward to fill vacant seats after Intermission, by which time it was assumed the rightful ticket holders wouldn't arrive. But Lydia loved to be up close to the music and hated to wait. She had become expert at occupying the empties at the beginning of the performance and had never been questioned before. "Are you sure?" She looked up slowly and smiled, hoping the diversion would grant her some time.

"No harm." His brown eyes were sharded with amber and smiled back in a way that made Lydia think he knew her secret. He had a high forehead, sandy hair, full lips, and slightly protruding ears. Like Stravinsky, Lydia thought, and bit her lip to keep from smiling. The crystals that dripped from the wall sconce behind the gentleman shot prisms of light around his head. "I'll just sit here." He settled into the adjacent vacant seat. "It's about to begin."

Lydia returned to her program, a flush deepening in her cheeks. She dried her moist palms on the velour seat cushion.

The gentleman set his elbow (forest-green herringbone, suede patch) on the armrest, unleashing the scent of apples and bed sheets, and there it remained when Lydia innocently raised her hand to turn the page and flicked her finger against his hand. He didn't start, didn't look, didn't even acknowledge the contact. She wondered whether to retreat, thereby surrendering the armrest for the duration of the performance, or whether to hold her ground and battle out the boundary during the first movement, when a second masculine voice interrupted.

"Excuse me," this one said, standing just beyond Lydia's neighbor and addressing them both. "But you're in our seats."

"Are we?" Lydia's neighbor asked.

"We've had the same ones for twenty years!" the man snapped, emphatically waving two tickets.

"Looks like we're busted," Lydia's neighbor said. By the time they crab-walked out from the center of the row and stood at the aisle to scout for two vacant seats, the lights had dimmed, and an usher escorted them from the auditorium.

"Exiled from Shostakovich," the man sighed. "May I buy you a drink? Champagne?" Lydia nodded. She watched him order from the bar in the reflection on the large plate glass windows, through which she could also see the plaza, with its trees wrapped in sparkly lights, and towers of water shooting up from a fountain. He returned with two flutes. "To Intermission and second chances," he said.

She clinked her glass to his. "To *The Rite of Spring*." Lydia drank, then cocked her head to listen to the muffled music from behind the paneled walls.

"Hmmm." He nodded and closed his eyes, listening, too.

When the piano's leisurely movement ended, she finally spoke. "My name is Lydia."

"Franklin."

They gravitated toward the bar for a second round, neither of them having much else to say. When the bartender, in an effort to kickstart their conversation, confessed he was an undertaker during the day and had once built a custom casket to house both a motorcycle enthusiast and his Harley, Lydia and Franklin laughed and quickly moved on to childhoods, books, and, skipping out on the symphony entirely, a surprisingly lovely session in bed.

A year later, Lydia and Franklin had merged their lives to include one address, a wall of books, a tasteful CD collection, and Johann, a goldfish Franklin had bought Lydia "just because." By fortuitous coincidence, the philharmonic was performing the same program he and Lydia had missed the night they first met. To celebrate the anniversary of their meeting, Franklin purchased second-row balcony tickets and supper at a tony downtown grill that specialized in tiny portions for the pre-concert crowd.

Franklin was garrulous over dinner, engaging the wine steward in conversation in a mixture of Italian and French, planning idyllic vineyard vacations that hinted suspiciously of honeymoons, asking whether Lydia preferred summer to spring, if she had ever crashed a symphony hall in Vienna, proclaiming her collarbones luscious, then gazing at her meaningfully over forkfuls of chicken Marsala.

Lydia's nape grew warm behind the collar of a new taupe blouse. Was Franklin going to ask her to marry him? They shared a chocolate crème brûlée for dessert, during which a staticky recording of a tin-pan piano and a jazzy blues singer begging "do me like you do" purred from the speakers. The queer song suddenly reminded Lydia of Lester. He was the one before Franklin, the one who made Lydia feel invisible by day and uninhibited at night. Lester held no promise for the future, nor did he ever pretend to. Even after eight months, he wouldn't let Lydia call him her boyfriend, wouldn't even show her his apartment.

When Lydia called Lester shortly after meeting Franklin to tell him their nighttime flings were history, he asked her to go out with him one last time. She impetuously agreed, then phoned Franklin to tell him she couldn't attend his mother's birthday party that night due to a migraine. As soon as she hung up, she ran out the door to meet Lester, without even bothering to brush her teeth or splash between her legs.

Once at the Prestige Inn, Lydia and Lester fell into bed without preamble. She was twelve, she was twenty; she was bad, she was good; she was shy, she was nasty; she was sweet, she was mean. It didn't matter how she was—Lester fucked her, with no distracting murmurs of love or charm. She left exhausted the next morning and threw herself into bed to soak up the last bit of fucking Lester before she had to dress to go to the movies with Franklin that night, who had left a message enquiring about her migraine before assuming she could keep their date.

Lydia had not heard from or even thought of Lester again, until now, until that song. She didn't miss him. Of course she didn't. Not when falling in love with Franklin was so easy. Easy and pleasant. Franklin was kind, dependable, educated, included Lydia in all aspects of his life, found her collarbones luscious, and, like Lydia, enjoyed the occasional breech in the social contract as long as no one really got hurt.

"Nice song," Franklin said, and purchased the CD on the way out to play in the car on the way to the philharmonic, which was now housed in a sumptuous new space, with stainless steel curves that made the building seem like a galleon prepared to set sail. By the time they were riding the escalator up to the lobby from the bowels of the parking structure, "do me like you do" was seared onto Lydia's brain, and her mood had progressed from a loathsome nostalgia for Lester to annoyed loathing for Franklin. What if he did propose? Could she say "yes" to a lifetime of pleasant and easy spiked with obsessive recollections of "do me like you do?"

They reached the lounge on the terrace, where Franklin went to buy cordials. Lydia looked out across the steel and glass atrium and shivered. She turned to see if Franklin had remembered to bring his gloves, and thought she saw him smiling at someone across the room, but when she looked to see whom, she saw only a woman in a red dress. The sort of woman Franklin wouldn't look at twice—wearing makeup that tried too hard—in a style of dress Franklin wouldn't care for: ill-fitting, flashing with rhinestones.

"Who's that?" Lydia asked when he returned.

"Who, darling?" he said, placing his hand on her waist. "Mmm, you're turning me on," he whispered close to her ear.

"No one." Lydia felt sad for the woman in the red dress, who chewed gum with her mouth open, swung her pocketbook on her hand a bit too wildly, and placed her hand over her mouth to stifle a belch that offended no one. A year ago, it had been Lydia standing alone before the performance, trying to savor the Kir Royale she desperately wanted to slug down; attempting to appear at ease in her solitary excursion. Lester would never have accompanied her, nor would she have wished him to.

The last bells chimed. Franklin took Lydia's plastic cup and tossed it into the trash. They walked to a side door marked "Orchestra," where a red-jacketed usher held up a gloved hand. "Tickets, please."

"Oh, we just want to go in for a look," Franklin said smoothly, waving his tickets in an absent-minded professorish way.

"Sorry, sir. You can look all you want," the usher said, staring him down behind her thick-lensed spectacles. "After the show." She appropriated his tickets and brought them close to, then far away from her eyes. "You're up at the top, sir. In the back. Let me escort you to your seats. They're just about to begin, and there's no late seating."

The usher led them up three flights of winding stairs covered in garish, floral wall-to-wall, then down a crooked hallway lined with glass. When they emerged from an ill-lit, oddly-angled passage and found themselves eye-level with the wooden ribcage of the auditorium's light scaffolding, Lydia felt like she had entered Alice's rabbit hole. She leaned over the rail to peer down onto the orchestra far below, nearly swooned, and fell back on her heels.

"We're in the belly of the whale," she said, and laughed to disguise the stars that swam in her eyes.

"It's all this Douglas fir. Makes you feel like you're inside a cello," Franklin said. "Will you look there?" He pointed down to the second row on the main floor, at two empty seats toward the center. "Waiting for us." He touched Lydia's hip to guide her down the steep stairwell. "We'll try again at Intermission," he whispered, then directed her to their row.

Focus, Lydia told herself, and found a point in the near distance, letting it become a beacon to help her maintain balance, a lighthouse to prevent her from toppling absurdly over the thin, burnished aluminum side rail into the open-lidded grand piano. Imagine the horror of that! A swan-like, headfirst dive with Lydia's meadow-colored skirt fluttering at her ankles until she hit the strings with a cacophonic screech, landed with the skirt flopped over her shoulders, and revealed to the audience that on the first anniversary of the most successful relationship she had ever been party to in her life, she had defiantly donned the most pathetic piece of underwear in the drawer—frayed and saggy, with shredded elastic. Lydia worried the panties signaled an underground act of rebellion. Did she unconsciously wish to undo her future with Franklin? And even so, hadn't the hints he dropped at dinner blasted that desire for the uprising into general disarray? What did she have against paradise anyway?

"Almost there," Franklin announced. "Seats thirty-nine and forty-one."

Lydia maintained course, grateful for the serene beacon, the lighthouse, which distracted her from the whirl of color, babble of conversations, honk-and-blurt of instruments, and intersecting planes of the walls around her that conjoined to create a precocious visual and aural screech. So determined was Lydia to stave off vertigo, it wasn't until she arrived at her assigned seat that she realized her lighthouse was not just a lighthouse: it was the toupee of the man in front of her.

And not just any toupee. This toupee seemed to have been fashioned from matted, bloodless roadkill. It was a dreadlock skullcap, a welcome mat of frizz. A hideous, frightful concoction that perched on its owner's head as though it owned him, not bothering to cover his hairless pate past the tops of his catcher's mitt ears, and leaving the eggshell skin on the back of his head naked and raw as a baby bird's.

The toupee's owner turned and looked up at Lydia. She abruptly cut her eyes away to a place just above it. To safer, higher ground. Make no mistake, this new spot promised. Lydia is not looking at your head. Or your hair. Whatever you call it. Your hat. Lydia is looking at me, this spot just above it. In fact, Lydia is so very much not noticing you or your hair, she's going to look you straight in the eye.

When she did, she saw eyes that glowed like shadowy lamps in a dark hall. Blue lights in velvet darkness, illuminating the way for stealth jets of insight. Eyes with a manic stillness that saw too much. Of everything. Pain. Wasted paper.

Lydia hovered halfway between standing and sitting, grimacing a smile. *I acknowledge you,* the smile relayed, *but not your extravagant hairpiece. I may sit just behind you, but our worlds orbit in opposite directions. Our ticket numbers are identical save for one letter, but we have nothing in common, nothing.*

Franklin was already seated. "Comfortable?" he asked, opening his program to find the length of the pieces, calculating their Intermission hustle to the restrooms and bar.

"Perfect," Lydia said. She sat and pulled her embroidered blazer about her shoulders. As she bent to stow her matching bag beneath her seat, she quietly breathed in her neighbor. He had no smell. None at all. He was neutral, as though he had no effect whatsoever on his surroundings, made no ripple in the pond.

Lydia settled back into her seat. The lights dimmed and the "Shostakovich Concerto in C Minor for Piano, Trumpet, and Strings, Op. 35" began. Lydia closed her eyes and slipped away on the opening flourish for trumpet and piano, then down into the broader, darker themes underscored by the strings and the solo trumpet's solemn, sustained notes.

His name was probably something like Alistair. He would speak softly. With a lisp. Perhaps an accent. Definitely orthodontic scaffolding hooked into pink gums, guarding soft palate, guiding crooked teeth into place. There was a general disregard for hygiene, which Lydia fact-checked in the smattering of dandruff across the shiny shoulders of last decade's gabardine. If she were to nudge his shoulder with her pump, he would turn around and apologize, and when they engaged in that full-on eye contact, she knew she would be locked into his gaze. If Alistair spoke, she would have no choice but to listen, for beneath the unfortunate skullcap no doubt was a razor-sharp intellect. She would be kind, witty; she would be free to flirt. He would be thankful for her attention; she would be beholden to his gratitude. Beneath his rayon and worn cotton vest beat a generous, true heart; a soul milled with passion and flair. The knowledge that she was one of the few who knew this would embolden her to laugh and (somehow, in her fantasy) place her hand on his thigh, which would be surprisingly hard from all the miles of walking he did, miles alone, and there would be a sharp intake of breath on both sides. A meaningful, long-lasting relationship was certain, for she would never be able to tear her gaze from his eyes, whose manic calm she now saw more clearly as the sparkling of a child or the knowing, impenetrable bead of a crow, and she was no longer ashamed of his mangled toupee. She would just call it a hat. Yes, a hat, and it was merely another part of him that she loved and indulged, like his penchant for radishes and glen-plaid vests, or his habits of rising to pee in the middle of the night and forgetting to buy new socks.

Lydia was wondering if Alistair wore his toupee during sex, when the first movement abruptly ended. She coughed discreetly along with the rest of the audience, who had been saving up throaty ejaculations since its beginning. Franklin offered Lydia a tissue and a lozenge, but she waved them away. When she realized she might have seemed annoyed, she grabbed Franklin's hand and pressed his knuckles to her lips, inserting the tip of her tongue between two fingers. He winked at her as the elegant moderato began its brief interlude.

Its simple eloquence made Lydia feel violently modern; she peeked to see if Alistair had noticed their wanton public display. Franklin was her treasure, Lydia knew this in her heart. Yet, as the violins swelled anew, tears sprang to her eyes, and her chest tightened with a suppressed sob. For how did she repay Franklin for his kindness and devotion?

First, she removed Alistair's clothes. He would want her to pair his mismatched socks and hang up the pants that didn't suit his jacket before she climbed onto him. She would refuse. Maybe even reprimand him for making such a request. Alistair's hands were soft, like a woman's, and she tied them to the bedposts with the long, silky scarves she reserved for chamber orchestra events. Alistair seemed frightened. And why not? What woman had ever captured him the way Lydia had? She reassured him with her eyes that he was in no danger, but no words issued from her mouth as she brought her lips to the velvety skin of his hard, muscular thighs.

Alistair moaned and writhed in response, his head twisting from side to side beneath the resolutely stationary toupee. Why won't he take it off when we make love? Lydia wondered. Didn't he know she would love him without it? What if she were to become obsessed with what was under there, or where it came from, and why? When she gently prodded him for information, Alistair would tease her at first.

"Who wants to know?" He'd smile over the rim of a chipped teacup and offer a basket of scones.

So she would stop asking, because she loved him, she loved scones, and if everything else was right in their world, there was no need to delve. But someday, maybe it would be after an argument, or the morning after a night of bad sleep, or maybe it would be a repercussion from an unfortunate dream of broken teeth, someday, the question would come up again. And after a while, Alistair would stop offering scones and become close-lipped and tight about his toupee, until one day Lydia would realize he's back in his own universe, he's let go of her gaze, he's shaken her off. And she wouldn't even care anymore, because she could no longer see the gleam of his eyes in the shadow of his snaggletooth and the smell of the radish breath, and it was all she could do not to suggest Head & Shoulders, and they would sadly shake hands and say goodbye. There'd be no fighting or bickering or name-calling or therapy, and Lydia would be sad but enlightened as she walked away and wondered why she couldn't just be happy the way she knew how to be back when she was able just to call it a hat.

Franklin's program crackled. Lydia watched him turn the page ever so slowly, in order to make the least possible noise, a practice which Lydia felt actually compounded the annoyance factor, a theory she and

Franklin had once debated so hotly that Lydia accidentally closed the car door on her hand and dissolved into tears in the parking structure, and Franklin put her fingers in his mouth to make them feel better.

The moderato drove into the final movement, fraught with madcap chases, a brilliant Spanish-sounding trumpet, and delicate pizzicato strings that buzzed under Lydia's skin like bees in a hive. He was still turning the goddamn page.

Lydia snatched his program, snapped the page shut, and slapped the book in Franklin's lap. Franklin gasped, and the row of heads immediately before them jerked and shushed in disapproval.

As soon as the clapping ended, Franklin rushed away to the men's room. Lydia followed leisurely. She would go to the ladies' room and then meet him at their prearranged spot. She flushed the toilet and wondered how couples managed to stay together for years and years; not only how but why? As she was washing her hands, Lydia noticed the sparkling red dress in the mirror over the basin next to her.

The woman caught Lydia's eye and smiled. Her top teeth protruded over her bottom lip in a way that was half beautiful and half beaver. Lydia smiled back, and watched from the corner of her eye as the woman applied bright red lipstick over those big, soft lips, which pressed together, then opened in a smile, revealing the terrible, amazing teeth.

"I saw you before with Franklin," Lydia imagined the too-red lips forming the words. "Does he still swing? Does he still take those crazy photographs?" The prospect was so thrilling and confusing, that Lydia found herself attempting to rinse soap from her hands three inches above the spigot. When she finally located the water, the ladies'-room door had shuddered and closed behind the woman. Lydia remained at the basin, where she applied frosted peach lipstick with dripping hands, threw away the tube of lipstick, and wiped her hands on her dress.

Lydia approached the bench in the courtyard next to the fountain that looked like a gigantic rubber-band ball, where Franklin chatted with the woman in red. Their shoulders touched as they laughed, and an air of intimacy pervaded, as obvious and overwhelming as the syrupy scent of night-flowering jasmine. "You were right, darling," he said when Lydia joined them, as he handed her champagne, in a real glass flute this time. "I was smiling at this woman earlier. I didn't realize that I recognized her, but I did. We're old friends. Janice, meet Lydia. Lydia, Janice."

"Old, old friends." Janice smiled her awful smile. "Franklin was just telling me how you met."

"Yes," said Lydia, stupidly.

"It sounds thrilling," said the too-red lips.

"We've waited a whole year for "The Rite of Spring." And if we're going to get into those orchestra seats this time, we should be going." Franklin grinned and slid his hand down the length of his silk tie, flipping up the end with a flourish.

"The idea of The Rite of Spring *came to me while I was still composing* Firebird," *Igor Stravinsky recalled, 45 years after the ballet's first performance in 1913. "I had dreamed of a scene of pagan ritual in which a chosen sacrificial virgin danced herself to death."* Franklin had secured the second-row seats, as promised. While he chatted up the usher about the use of material on the grantors' wall, Lydia slipped by, then pretended to need assistance removing her wrap. Now, head down, studying her program, heart percussing wildly in her chest, throat, and ears, Lydia found herself reading the same sentences over and over. All she could think of were

the words she had put in that woman's—Janice? Janet?—mouth: "Does Franklin still swing?" "Does he still take those crazy photographs?" *The evocative opening, with the bassoon playing in its highest register, immediately transports the listener to some vague, primeval past as Stravinsky conjures what he described as "a sort of pagan cry."*

The music crashed and thundered with jarring percussion and offbeat rhythms. Lydia's mind leapt to one possible future. Some Saturday afternoon, with her husband Franklin out returning videos and Lydia home in her pajamas, holding a fan of glossy Polaroids of anonymous body parts, red, shiny, engorged; opened and spread by manicured fingers, wrists with gold watches. Quick! What kind of watch did Franklin wear? A brown leather band. Was it cracked? Crocodile? A gold face. She really had no idea and was more ashamed for not knowing the kind of watch her husband wore than she was for going through the photos in the manila envelope that she'd imagined she'd found in the drawer behind his shorts.

Franklin had a right to his sex life before he met her, of course he did. They were adults! But these! She studied each photo carefully, dreading the next for fear that he'd be there, her Franklin, naked but for a pointy party hat and those sport socks he favored, surrounded by a harem of housewives, nuzzling his neck or energetically bouncing their heads above his cock. Lydia might understand if they were beautiful women, models or porn stars or strippers or whores, who represented fantasies that Lydia herself could never achieve. Would never even *want* to achieve! But to think that Franklin partied with—was that the proper term?— "swung" with regular people like themselves, was unfathomable to Lydia. She imagined a PTA meeting of parents and teachers, then removed all their clothes, put gin and reefer into their hands, and watched as they screeched and howled and paired off in groups of twos and threes to grunt and moan and spill drinks and burn holes in bad orange carpeting. For some reason, they always wore hats and shoes; she could never make them all the way naked.

She held her breath as she flipped to the next photograph, and because it was her fantasy, her worst nightmare came true. Here were Franklin and Janice/Janet, not just together, not just naked, not just wearing hats and shoes and drinking cocktails from Dixie cups, wearing cracked, brown leather watches and too-red lipstick, not just ignoring receding hairlines and long teeth, saggy, lopsided breasts and stretch marks, heat rashes from thigh rubbing and carpet burns, but holding hands, dammit!, and smiling.

The music was wild and stark. She peeked at Franklin and was surprised when she found him watching her and smiling. She laid her head on his shoulder and, through her lashes, searched for Alistair's toupee, her beacon, in the row far above the orchestra where they had sat during the first half. She imagined a young woman in a wooded glade, encircled by bears and other beasts; dancing, dancing, dancing, until she dropped.

GNEISS

· · · · ·

She and Gary hadn't arrived at the B&B, but Jennifer was prepared to hate it. You never knew what kind of baroque fantasy you were getting yourself into. Chintz. Chihuahuas. Oil portraits of forebears with chimp brows and weak chins. A dust-moted parlor with tea service in cozies. Theme-laden brunches (*Pirates & Pancakes! Autumnal Omelets!*). Rooms filled with posies and cabbage flowers and lace.

"What about this?" Gary asked, adjusting the rear view mirror. He'd been practicing his toast since they drove through Banning a half hour back, which was when Jennifer first announced she had to pee and he had requested an emergency rating on a scale of one to ten. "I first noticed Angela when we were freshman at UCLA. Her hair was so blue…"

Jennifer, who was only at stage three, megaphoned her hands around her mouth. "How blue was it?" As if a B&B weekend weren't torture enough, it was compounded by having to attend the wedding of Gary's best friend Angela, who had the blazing she-balls to make Gary her *Man of Honor*.

"Never mind," he said. He turned up the volume on the one station with reception out in Bumfucksville.

Jennifer flicked her window up and down to the beat of a Journey song for its entire length. She had always wondered whether he and

Angela were lovers back then. When she'd asked (and she had, more than once), he'd always claimed their friendship *wasn't like that.* Still, it needled her, especially because Angela's wedding was such a Big Thing. Unlike Jennifer and Gary's wedding, which was a decidedly Unbig Thing. It was an Anti Thing, practically a No Thing, something they kept intimate by simply applying for the license and pronouncing themselves married over sushi, congratulating each other on shared views that flipped the finger in the face of tradition.

"I'm closing in on seven," she said, when the song was over, although really she was only at five.

"Hang on for ten minutes," he said. "And quit with the window. You're wasting perfectly good air conditioning."

Jennifer knew Gary was nervous about the wedding and how much he hated being late for anything. But she was fussing for a fuck or a fight, and it couldn't be helped. It wasn't her fault she didn't have a *morning dress* in her closet, which is what Angela requested the ladies wear to both the rehearsal and Victorian-style nuptials. *Good god.*

Gravel crunched under the tires as they finally rolled into the parking lot of the Chanticleer Villa in Twenty-nine Palms. Jennifer jumped out and headed down the purple-stoned path, under the lilac arbor toward the stone mansion with the kitschy gingerbread trim painted turquoise blue as if to warn of the Navajo crap on the gift carousel inside.

She opened the door and a little bell went *tingaling.* She pulled off her sunglasses to let her eyes adjust to the dark foyer and toggled the light switch to let whomever wasn't greeting her after her long desert sojourn know she had arrived. There was neither chintz nor Chihuahua in sight.

The reception area walls were white, with tufts and hillocks of stucco sticking up like meringue. An index card was taped to the cash register: "Wine and cheese, if you please – 5 to 7 p.m." There was no sign of Navajo crap. A glass-doored hutch displayed wooden discs, ranging in size from coaster to dinner plate and topped with glass domes. Under one was a loose ball of dirty red thread. Bits of animal skin with cowlicks of mottled gray fur lay under another. A clump of blond hair like you'd find in a shower drain (not if you were Jennifer; definitely if you were Angela). A half-rotted, shiny eggplant that appeared freshly lacquered. A rodent-like animal—a mole?—at rest, eyes frozen open, with tiny paws pressed together as in prayer and pink cotton batting extruding from a wound in its side. *What the hell?* Jennifer reached out to open a door but stopped when a man appeared at the reception desk.

At least she thought he was a man. The crew cut, apple cheeks and thin maroon lips above a neck soft with flesh reminded her of a photo she'd once seen of Gertrude Stein. "Good afternoon," Gertrude said. The voice was neither masculine nor feminine; just pleasant, like water on rocks.

"Jennifer and Gary Brand. With the wedding. Two nights."

Gertrude tucked rimless spectacles behind both ears and ran a finger down the register book page. "Ah, yes. The others arrived hours ago. The shuttle's already gone to the lodge." A fine netting of lines crisscrossed her or his cheeks, forehead and chin.

"Believe me, I know," Jennifer said. Laughter sounded from the parking lot, where the Man of Honor was gesticulating, gabbing on his cell.

Gertrude gestured for Jennifer to follow outside, which she did, scanning for telltale signs of sexuality or gender (she would settle for ilk): eyelashes, stubble, a bra clasp, boxer short lines, pink socks. What would pink socks mean really anyway? Both she and Gary had a favorite pair.

Still talking, the Man of Honor waved as they crossed the parking lot. He pointed to the trunk of their car. Jennifer pointed at Gary, who pointed to Gertrude. Jennifer pointed more forcefully at her husband, who raised a despairing arm into the air. She shrugged and shouted, "We should have stopped in Banning." He stuck a finger in his free ear and turned away. Jennifer trotted to catch up with Gertrude, who had stopped to wait in a courtyard by a fountain that poured into a faux lagoon.

"There used to be three," Gertrude said, glowering at two spotted koi, their heads thrust above water, mouths dumbly gaping. "But we have owlets." Gertrude squinted, pointing to the top of a palm tree where golden eyes glowed in the shadow of a frond. "The mama likes to go fishing at dusk."

"What's that stuff in the reception area?" Jennifer's nose wrinkled; she couldn't help it. "The hair, the roadkill, the vegetables."

"Gifts from a lady friend," Gertrude said, illuminating nada.

Jennifer suddenly remembered she'd had to pee for a very long time.

The bungalow wasn't as bad as it could have been (not as bad as Jennifer hoped it would be), but it was no Shangri-La. Maybe for someone with an ivy fetish. There were plastic garlands around the curtain rods. Stenciled vines along the ceiling. A hand-painted mural of the stuff tumbling down a rock wall onto the actual headboard and walls on both sides of the bed.

In the bathroom, Jennifer noted the ivy-printed tiles along the woodland creature-footed tub (not the typical lion paws, dragon feet or clawed talons but something cloven and vaguely diabolical). She re-entered the bedroom, where the Man of Honor was reclining on the bed's ivy-printed comforter. She wanted to tell him about Gertrude's House of Weird Stuff in reception, about the survival struggle of koi versus owl.

Gary tapped at his laptop, his eyes boring into the screen. "Feeling better?" he asked, not looking up.

"Than what?" She knew that posture, the way he hunched over the keyboard. If she spoke now, he wouldn't listen. If they could just *do it* before dinner, Jennifer was certain she'd be rid of the prickly feeling she'd had under her skin ever since she zipped up her suitcase full of inappropriate clothes. She tore off her jeans and T-shirt and jumped up and down on the bed in her panties and bra.

"*Jennifer.*"

"*Gary.*" Little ivy leaflets were daubed on the globe of the ceiling lamp.

You're making it hard to type," he said, finally looking up. "What are you doing?"

"What are *you* doing?" she repeated, then sighed melodramatically. She climbed down and wrapped herself in an ivy-patterned spa robe.

Gary's typing accelerated. He was going in for the majestic finish, the sunset cloudburst, the star-spangled wildebeest. "Just finishing up Angela's toast. I made her a bet that she'd cry," he said. The computer chimed "adios" as he closed it. "If we hurry, we'll still make the appetizers. I hear the sweetbread croquettes are killer." He was up and stripping and in the bathroom already, the shower roaring.

Tonight's dinner was to be a Victorian Thanksgiving feast, with oysters, sweetbreads, roast duck, a turkey, mince pies; twelve courses in all. Jennifer unfurled her slinky halter dress from the suitcase and put it on. It looked great on her, and she in it, and the dry desert heat made her normally frizz-tending hair lie lank. Fuck Angela's sweetbread croquettes.

Fuck her fantasy wedding and her honeymoon with what's-his-name to build organic vegan homes for cash-poor, coffee-rich Guatemalans. What *was* his name? Jennifer met him once. Twice. He'd come to their home. She'd overcooked the fish.

Gary came out of the bathroom, shaking his shirt around his shoulders, knotting his ascot.

"I can't believe she got you to wear an ascot," Jennifer said.

He caught her eye in the mirror as he pulled on his tailcoat and popped open his top hat, both last-minute thrift store finds in which Jennifer had to admit he looked delicious.

"You're treating her like she's a queen or something. If you were so important to her, she would have put us up at the lodge with everyone else in the wedding party."

"We would have gotten a room at the lodge if you didn't wait so long to RSVP," Gary said. "We already talked about this."

Jennifer couldn't stop; part of her was really good at rehashing the hash. "Maybe if you slept with her in college, we would have gotten a nice room at the lodge."

Gary's shoulders sagged and he turned to look at Jennifer. "Angela's my friend. This is her day. If you're going to ruin it, you'd best just not come."

"Fine." She pulled off the dress, flung it to the floor and jumped into the bed, folding her arms across her chest.

"Fine," he said, buckling his belt as he stepped into his loafers. "What will you eat?"

"Wine and cheese, if I please," she said.

Gary kissed her turned cheek and grabbed his laptop. "I'll bring you a plate," he said. "And I'll call if I'm going to be late."

"For your very important date," she said.

"Sometimes, I swear," he said, and closed the door.

She got up and paced around the room. A brochure on the desk caught her eye: "Rock Formations in the California Desert." She scanned the first paragraph. "Gneiss (pronounced 'nice') is a common type of rock formed by metamorphic processes from pre-existing formations that were originally either igneous or sedimentary rocks." She put the brochure back where she found it, leaped under the covers and punched the pillow on his side of the bed. She didn't really care who Gary slept with ten years ago. So why did she keep bringing it up?

■ ■ ■ ■ ■

Jennifer napped dreamless and hard, then awoke ravenous. She felt crappy about being a pill and wondered what course Gary and the wedding party were drunkenly devouring over at the lodge. She put on sweats and a T-shirt to go visit the big house, then threw on the spa robe, hoping she might slip a bottle of chardonnay into its giant pocket to bring back to the bungalow. After all that dinner and drink, Gary might be feeling frisky. As she set out across the parking lot, she noticed a path she hadn't seen earlier. It was nicely shaded, so she followed it into a glade of birch trees.

Coin-shaped leaves flashed silver in the soft breeze as they grabbed whatever bits of light dappled in. She stopped to admire the light, the green. She'd been cooped up so long. In the house. At work. In her can't-shut-it-up head. There was a large boulder nearby, broken almost exactly in half. She wiped dust from the flat surface to expose a layer of white granite in the center, shaped like a lopsided heart. She couldn't help but grin and made a note to show it to Gary. Maybe tonight, pre-frisk, she'd bring him out here and just point. Things could go on from there.

She sat on the rock and noticed the top of a sapling—maybe ten feet tall, trunk six inches across—had been drawn down and tucked under a log, creating an arch. *How strange.* She was thinking about wine and cheese when from behind her came a loud snap. She turned just in time to see a tree newly cracked and bent at the waist, its crown crashing groundward. She looked around to see what had caused the break. An animal? Dry lightning? But there was nothing, no sound at all, as though even the trees were holding their breath. The back of her neck felt suddenly light, as though separate from the weight of her body.

The dining room of the Chanticleer Villa had no oil portraits of Neanderthal ancestors. No miniature dogs. Not even a piano. Just simple white walls with that meringue stucco, dark Spanish furniture and a stone fireplace so big you could walk inside it. Jennifer stood alone at the buffet, sampling two-handedly straight from the serving trays. There were dates stuffed with Roquefort, prosciutto-wrapped melon, and pesto-flaked shrimp, chased with a zesty red from a plastic wine glass. A far cry from the simply stated "wine and cheese."

She threw a couple more of everything onto a plate and wandered the bookshelves along the far wall. Old clothbound classics, Thackeray, Shakespeare, Eliot. She vaguely remembered *Mill on the Floss* from freshman English, the brother and sister drowning in an underwater embrace. She tiptoed to peer over swinging doors into a kitchen with dark cabinets and white countertops. Red pots and pans simmered on an industrial-sized stove; their non-working friends hung on a metal grid suspended from the ceiling. A postcard was thumbtacked to the inside of one of the swinging doors. "Bigfoot Says Hi!" in block letters, in the style of a vintage fruit-crate label. She had a stabbing desire to read the back of the card. Her fingernail had just slipped under the head of the tack when the light in the room darkened and a shadow crossed the window above the sink. Was it Gertrude? The wind? Maybe Gary had come back from the dinner early. Perhaps it was nothing, but Jennifer suddenly felt unalone. Her gooseflesh convinced her to leave the postcard post haste and go pour another plastic glass of wine.

Gertrude sat on a bench in the courtyard. His eyes were closed. Binoculars rested at his feet. Jennifer didn't want to intrude, so she sat on the bench directly across. The Moroccan tile fountain rose in three levels. Polished stones—all shades of blue, from indigo to sky—lined its edges. The koi gaped at her with popped, hungry eyes. Fairy lights circled the trunks of the palm trees. A white rabbit, a stuffed toy, was nailed to one behind Gertrude, quasi-crucified ten feet above ground.

Jennifer wondered if Gertrude could feel her looking at him.

Gertrude opened his eyes.

Jennifer pointed at the rabbit. "What's that?" The wine made her ask.

"Something to amuse my lady friend," he said, smiling. "The owl's nest is on this side. You can see better from here." He patted the bench. "Come."

Jennifer sat next to Gertrude and noted he smelled faintly of garlic, blue cheese and pesto. Now was her chance. "My name's Jennifer," she said, then gulped wine and held it in her mouth. She was ready for anything. Sally/Sam. George/Julie. Ned/Nina.

"Francis," he said, knocking her back to square one. "You didn't go to the dinner?"

Jennifer almost said, *No, female trouble,* thinking it might elicit more details, but decided to let it go. What did it matter? She shook her head and swallowed.

Francis picked up the binoculars. "She's about to come out." With his free hand, he tossed some raw cubed meat a few feet away from their bench.

The mother owl swooped. The size of a human infant, she snatched the beef and ascended to the top of the palm with a single flap of her immense wings, creating a gust of wind with the motion and a sound Jennifer promised herself she would try to never forget. Which reminded her. "A tree broke in the forest today and I heard it," she said.

"Really?" Francis put down the binoculars and looked at her. His eyes were steel gray, like his brush cut. Almost bullets. Above, the owlets screeched and mewled as they fed.

Jennifer took Francis into the glade and pointed to the broken tree. "I heard it crack, then fall, then nothing else," she said. "Absolute silence. What could have caused it?"

Francis wrapped both hands around the trunk. He was handsome when he smiled. Or pretty. "Where were you when it happened?"

Jennifer pointed at the boulder with the heart. "Right there."

"That's a lovely specimen, isn't it? There's a pamphlet about some of the rock formations here in the escritoire in your room." He said the French word like an American would, es-kreet-twah, *which was the right way for an American to say it,* Jennifer thought. "See the white heart in the middle? That's called gneiss. From the old German meaning 'to spark or glitter,' but also from the Saxon word for 'decay.' One of those either/or kinds of things." He bent down and scratched at some dirt near the broken tree trunk, then crooked his finger at her.

"Was this there when it happened?" He held a blue stone in his ser-
rated palm.

"No way," Jennifer said. "I would have seen it."

"Did you bring it here?"

No again.

Francis pressed it into her hand. "I think my lady friend likes you."

Jennifer looked into Francis's eyes. She couldn't tell if the heat was
from his hand or the stone.

The white marble countertop made the blue stone bluer. Unnaturally
blue, which made it all the more beautiful. Francis cracked eggs against
a red mixing bowl. He was on his second glass of wine from a bottle he
had fetched from the cellar and wiped carefully with a linen towel. "You
should have seen this place before we fixed it up," he said as he selected a
whisk from the rack above his head and rinsed it. "What a wreck. But the
first time we laid eyes on it, we knew we had to have it. We knew exactly
how we'd paint the rooms, how we'd plant the garden, how we'd handle
the extreme heat and cold. We got pretty far, too, before Jamie passed and
moved on. We finished the whole place except for your little bungalow. I
just haven't had the..." He stopped to search for the word.

"Heart?" Jennifer asked.

"Energy." When Francis whisked, his entire body moved—butt, belly,
goiter. He sucked in his cheeks, concentrating as he poured the mixture
into a pan over flame.

Jennifer cut a wedge of cheese off a sweating wheel and pressed it to a
piece of bread. She studied a black and white photograph of Francis with
his partner Jamie, who was a woman or a man just like Francis. They were
standing in the courtyard, the fountain in pieces, the lagoon still a trench.

Francis held a trowel overhead in victory. His cheeks were flushed pink and he looked very young and happy. Jamie grinned, a cocktail umbrella between the teeth, one foot propped up on a bag of cement. A vague unfocused blot hovered above Jamie's head against the background of birch trees, as though someone had tried to erase a bit of the image. As though someone or something was peering through the silver branches. Jennifer wondered if right now, in their Victorian get-ups, in the middle of whatever course they were on, Angela and what's-his-name were as happy as Jamie and Francis looked back then. If she and Gary were that happy, too.

Francis flipped the omelet into the air, caught it underhanded with a plate, and set it in front of Jennifer. She stared into its eggy beauty, the beads of oil glistening on its surface, browned patches creating a calico effect. Francis sat across from her and held the photo up in front of his face like a compact mirror. "Two years—no, it must be three now—after Jamie died, I'd see shadows outside the windows. Then came the gifts. You know, at reception? I thought Jamie was haunting me."

"I saw something, too! As though the light changed!" Jennifer began to eat faster.

"Yes," Francis smiled. "It can happen like that." He filled their glasses with more wine. "Then one weekend, a strange man checked in. Said he was looking for Bigfoot."

"Igfoo?" Jennifer repeated; hot egg fell from her mouth.

Francis nodded as though he couldn't believe he said it himself. "He heard there'd been some sightings out here. I didn't tell him anything about anything, but he told me a lot about Bigfoot."

"Like what?"

"Oh, like how strong and fast they are. How they move silently through dense brush. Or tuck the tips of young trees under rocks to make arches with no purpose at all. Their sense of humor. Like today. Cracking that tree in half." Francis giggled. "That's when I knew it wasn't Jamie that was visiting. It was a Bigfoot. I call her my lady friend. Sounds more personable."

"Have you ever seen your...lady friend?"

"I haven't *seen* seen her," Francis said. "But she visits when I'm lonely. She has this, I don't know, power. Hits right here." He thumped his chest. "Makes you soft inside." He shrugged.

Jennifer didn't know whether to laugh at his story or debunk his theory or tell him sometimes she imagined Gary dead and gone after some unremarkable and painless death, and she was miserable, just miserable without him. "I love this omelet," is what she said.

And it was true, she did. She also loved the butter lettuce dressed with Dijon. She loved the wine and the cheese and the blue stone and almost Francis and even a little bit Jamie for his goofy, umbrella'd smile and for making Francis's cheeks shine. She wished she and Gary would fall in love with a place that made them want to make it beautiful, make it their own. She even loved a little bit Angela and what's-his-name for having their stupid wedding at this cockamamie place.

For dessert, Francis served a warm apple tart that almost made her cry.

· · · · ·

Jennifer watched the glow of Francis' flashlight among the trees. She thought she heard him murmuring, possibly praying. Or talking to his lady friend. Or to Jamie. Or maybe it was just birds. Those owls. There was a message from Gary on her cell phone. "There's a bit of a situation here," he said. "Dexter got hammered and needs help. I'm gonna get him to bed and sleep on the floor in his room. See you in the morning."

Dexter. Of course! She dragged a chair from inside the bungalow and parked it on the porch outside, then found the brochure on the escritoire. She used a flashlight to read about gneiss, monzogranite pileups, magma and granite cracks. When the night air grew cool, she brought out the duvet cover, tucked it under her chin, and wondered whose room Gary was really passed out in. She wondered if Angela had cried at his toast, if the sweetbread croquettes were indeed killer. She decided if Gary and Angela had been lovers way back when, it didn't matter now. She leaned back. There were too many falling stars to count. She fell asleep with the blue stone in her hand.

"Did you get my message?" Even though the sun had not completely risen above the hills behind him, Gary was wearing sunglasses, the special pair that made him look European and which he saved for particularly hungover mornings. His frock coat was wrinkled; his top hat, minus its brim. "Did you sleep outside?"

"Yes and yes," Jennifer said, stretching. "Gosh, I'm thirsty."

He jogged to retrieve something from the front seat of his car, which was now covered in a fine layer of grit. When he got back, he removed the cap from the bottle of Voss and drank, then offered the bottle to Jennifer. "My speech made Angela cry, so I won the bet. Now she owes us dinner. The food was amazing. We'll have to go to the lodge together some time."

"Bottled at an artesian source in the pristine wilderness of Southern Norway," she read on the back of the bottle. She felt the familiar prickle at the back of her neck. Designer water was one of her favorite rants.

"Sorry if I was short with you yesterday." Gary sat on the arm of her chair and kissed the top of Jennifer's head. "I was just rattled about the speech and everything. It's nice to be out of town though, isn't it?"

"Yes," she said, then took a long drink.

"Does it taste like it comes from Norway?" he asked, then fell backward across her lap. "Or maybe it has the bouquet of a northern clime."

She drank, swished it in her mouth and swallowed. "They're ripping you off," she said. "This water tastes just like that vintage from Iceland."

Gary laughed. "Dexter went overboard on the champagne. He accused me and Angela of being lovers, to which we both said impossible, but he wouldn't shut up and practically challenged me to a duel. The wedding, if it's still on, should be interesting."

"I'll bet," Jennifer said, and she knew he knew there was no rancor.

"I'm so glad we got married the way we did," he said, looking out at the small glade. "Last night turned out to be a circus." He looked back to Jennifer. "Angela said there's a great thrift store in town if you wanted to look for a dress."

"Sounds fun," she said. "I'll have to check it out."

"I need a shower." Gary said, then grunted as he curled up and hopped to his feet. "And so do you." He held out his hand and winked.

Jennifer stood next to him and felt heat across her chest. Too much wine last night. Or too much cheese. The sun higher over Gary's shoulder. Maybe Francis's lady friend. Or maybe just Gary, in his wrinkled white shirt with the stained armpits, wanting her. Wanting him. "Look at those rocks over there," she spun around, pressing her back against his chest.

Jennifer wanted to tell him she thought the rocks looked like there was an alligator trapped inside the planet, and its tail was whipping around, punching at the earth's surface, making it bulge and split, the giant lizard inside thrashing and fighting to burst free of its cage, and the heat and everything pressing on it: hunger, thirst, desire. Instead, she said, "That's a monzogranite pileup caused by the upheaval of magma. When the top layers of dust fall away, it's called gneiss."

"Your hair looks nice," he said, and turned her around. His breath was close, great and slow, like owl wings.

SPONTANEOUS LIGHT

· · · · ·

For the third time in as many nights, the hallway light snapped on of its own volition. Mindy awoke and searched the weak glow that spilled into her bedroom from the hall. The first night it happened, she had lain frozen in repose, listening with her entire body for the sound of footsteps and creaking boards, or someone shuffling through the drawers in her kitchen desk. She sniffed the air for unfamiliar cologne, then made a puffing noise. No man had ever entered this house; any cologne would be unfamiliar. Fists clenched, chest taut, she waited for something to happen, until fear's fatigue toppled her back to sleep. The second night, she wondered if the tiny house was haunted, and tracked the air for brimstone or whatever dank, meatish odor might announce a spectral event. This time she brazenly raised herself from bed, eyes closed, lumbered into the hallway, and toggled the sticky switch until the house was dark again. The globe on the ceiling-mounted fixture shone with faint heat, and doves trailed garlands of flowers from their beaks around its molding at the base.

Back under the covers—hipspread located, toeholds found—Mindy was awake with her thoughts: nickering, nervous thoroughbreds with red, rolling eyes. (She was afraid of the dark. She was afraid of the light.)

Took-took-took! A peculiar, reedy noise outside the window halted Mindy's litany. She braced for calamity and drew back the child's blanket she had tacked up for privacy when she moved in and never bothered to replace. The owls were *hoo-hooing* on a low-hanging branch, wings flapping like sails, murmured blurts overlapping, flaunting their congress with the exuberance of randy motel patrons. Mindy banged on the window, exhaling only after the birds pulled apart and catapulted through the whispering needles like dark, heavy knives. (She was afraid of nests. She was afraid of knives.) Mindy's catalogue finally lulled her to sleep.

That morning Mindy fell into her daily routine. Fill the kettle. Grind the beans. Check the clock. It was now over a year that she had signed over custody. (She was afraid to remember. She was afraid to forget.) She stirred in cream and sugar, opened the sliding glass door, and stepped onto her small wooden balcony. Her cabin was tucked in the forested pocket of a dead-end street. She drank from her mug, scouring the placid blue sky for imminent danger (She was afraid of helicopters. She was afraid of smoke.) and suddenly remembered last night's dream, in which she and her ex-husband, Chris, became owls. Owl Chris flapped and hopped about, crowing over a recently captured ground squirrel: "Who's the best provider, baby? Who? Who?" Questioned Mindy's whereabouts: "I came home to the tree last night and couldn't find you, you." Criticized the way she cared for their daughter, Shannon: "I've seen better mothers in a zoo, zoo."

Inside, Mindy washed her mug and shed her robe to shower. She had long ago abandoned the mirror, with its betrayal of reflection. Pouches the color of eggplant above her cheeks. Tiny blond whiskers above her lip. Thighs striped with stretch. Hot water pounded her shoulders in the awkward, mint-colored stall, and the soap's chemical scent conjured a series of fleet images that followed organically, like seasons. Her tongue tracing the plum-colored birthmark inside Chris's thigh during the heat of their initial passion. The blue vinyl of the passenger door when he roughed her that time, windows steamy against the slap of rain. The curveball surprise of conception, a quickening both inside and out as plans and promises were made, unmade, then made again on Zuma beach with the wind lashing her hair against her cheeks until they buzzed from stinging. Mindy adored her pregnancy, gratefully floating in hormone-induced serenity, letting Chris make decisions, her mind peaceful, her slumber deathlike. Then came the child, like a tiny alien, and the pins and needles of sleep deprivation and motherhood. Chris instinctively knew how to calm Shannon, whether to let her suckle his thumb or to rock her, leaving Mindy to squint over how-to books with a highlighter, dreading the next stage, the next test. Mindy counted the days before she could return to work, secretly scratching small notches with her thumbnail in the wood frame of the bathroom door. An inch equaled a week, four inches a month. The child grew daily, each day becoming more like Chris, more herself, and less her mother.

Mindy erased the images with a cool rinse before dressing, left a message for the landlord about the erratic light switch, and double-checked all the locks on the windows before buckling in for the cross-town commute.

Her street was mined with newly trenched holes and humps and loud metal plates—a Public Works Department project to rehabilitate the 40-year-old sewer lines. Men in fluorescent vests stood waist-high in the ground, brandishing shovels and cell phones. At the summit of a vertigo-steep hill, a third man with a stop sign waved her down. A large yellow

Caterpillar dangling an oversize concrete donut was inching backwards to drop it into a ditch on the other side of the road. Mindy jerked her emergency brake and started to sweat. (She was afraid her steering wheel might snap off in her hands. She was afraid of the smell of her body.) The donut sent her thoughts back to another time.

· · · · ·

It was Friday afternoon at the museum office where Mindy managed the printing of the monthly newsletter. Her relish for organization and mastery of order enabled last-minute program changes, image updates, and copy corrections to flow from desk to desk without typical deadline-day chaos. Her newsletter had never been late. It was after six when Mindy handed over the final discs to the printer. Shannon was still waiting at preschool. As if propelled by an unseen force, Mindy spent the next hour driving, devising an improvised grid of fences and lawns, vans and sedans, imagining Chris's reaction to her negligence. When she finally pulled into their brick-lined drive, Chris was waiting on the front lawn. Shannon was on the porch, chattering to the contents of her Happy Meal.

Chris was red with fury, hands trembling at his sides. "The school had to call my sister again. I can't believe you let this happen."

Let this happen, Mindy thought. When she got out of the car, Chris grabbed her shoulders and shook her until her ponytail shook loose. *Punish me*, she thought. *I deserve this*. He pulled his hand back to strike her, but stopped, and shook his head. Chris walked to the porch and swung Shannon inside the house, leaving Mindy exposed on the lawn.

Mindy made her way into the kitchen and stared into the drain at the sink, unable to breathe until she focused on her roses in the side yard, shocking with their untimely blood-red blooms. She could hear Chris bathing Shannon, the girl's loud voice joyfully delivering a nonsensical narrative of monsters and goats. Mindy went outside and clipped a small bouquet. On her return, she noticed a foil-wrapped paper plate on the front porch. Under the foil were rice and beans, a circle halved in brown and orange. She took in the beans with the roses, scraped them into the disposal, and tossed away the lard-soaked plate. The roses made a lovely centerpiece, but when Chris packed two bags and left with Shannon to spend the night at his sister Karen's, Mindy threw them into the trash as well.

· · · · ·

The car behind her honked, and the man in the orange vest was waving with both hands. Mindy released the brake, even though she still couldn't see around the Caterpillar, and gripped the steering wheel, palms slick. The man in the vest waved again, this time impatiently, scowling. Mindy accelerated, descending toward downtown. (She was afraid of head-on collisions. She was afraid of running over a dog.) Finally she emerged from the hills and turned onto Sunset Boulevard. Normally there was a snarl of traffic here, with cars migrating from intersection to inter-section in clumps. But today green lights stretched down the scorched boulevard as far as Mindy could see. Something must be going on. (She was afraid of bomb threats and police activity.) Mindy succumbed to the seductive hum of the tires on asphalt, the gentle rocking as she swayed around potholes, and splashes of tar expelled up from the river of meth-ane gas running just below the surface of the street. This same mixture of gas and asphalt created the La Brea Tar Pits, a lake of muck that created a death trap for the hideous prehistoric beasts that roamed the L.A. Basin tens of thousands of years ago. It was a museum now.

Mindy hated museums and considered it a great personal achievement that she could actually work in one now, though it housed art and not human figures cast in wax. Mindy had a specific terror of wax museums ever since she visited one as a child. The exhibits themselves were dramatically lit and the passageways pitch dark, with tiny floor lights that gleamed like dim stars to keep the visitors from stumbling into the displays. After covering her eyes through the bloody Chamber of Horrors, with its tortured heads and sawed-in-half man, Mindy had somehow become separated from her mother in the crowds that pushed through Frontier History. At five years, maybe six, she had her wits enough about her to remain in place until her mother came to find her. She waited for what seemed like hours, studying a mother Indian with a baby strapped to a board on her back roasting a small animal above a campfire. The father, a chief in a magnificent headdress, stared off into the nearby forest, a crude axe in one hand. Mindy stood between two starry guideposts, her heart thumping yet calmed by the details of the scene—the crying baby on the board, the glistening flesh of the meat, the father's cruel hooked nose, his elegant train of feathers. Suddenly, the father—a real person planted among the wax characters—raised his axe and turned his head, black eyes blazing directly into hers. Mindy's body felt as though it might burst. She swallowed her scream, just as her mother returned to find Mindy terrified and paralyzed, humiliated in the puddle of now-cooling wet at her feet.

Mindy grabbed a box of tissues from the glove compartment, turned up the radio and cried all the way to the office.

·····

The morning after the beans was chilly and gray. When Chris brought Shannon home after breakfast, Mindy was already in the side yard, studying her roses. He asked her to watch Shannon for a few hours—he had to wrap up some things at the office—and wondered if they could have dinner that night at Clancy's; Karen would babysit. Mindy agreed, but her stomach tightened at the prospect. (She was afraid of public scenes. She was afraid of trendy crowds.) Shannon cried when Chris left. Mindy gathered her up and rocked her on the porch glider for what seemed like hours, until Mindy's arms went prickly, then dead. Mindy saw Chris in her daughter's eyes, felt his criticism in the child's cloudy, unwavering gaze. *Would I love her better if she looked more like me?* When the sun finally broke through and Shannon had hiccupped herself silent, Mindy left her in the netted pen on the enclosed porch and delved into the roses. She mapped out her strategy—dig, nip, prune, twine—and went to work. (She was afraid of powdery mildew. She was afraid of black spots and rust.) By the time she tore off her gloves—sweating and satisfied—the chill had returned. A shriek reminded Mindy of her charge, and as she rounded the side yard, she was shocked to see Shannon cavorting with strangers. Mindy lurched toward them. "Shannon!" Why wasn't Chris here, to see how she couldn't be trusted?

Shannon was clutching the hand of a stocky woman with red-brown skin, a long black braid, tight acid-washed jeans, and brightly embroidered slippers. Another girl, the woman in miniature, held the other. The trio skipped in a loop as the woman sang in Spanish. At the end of the song, they heaped to the ground, the little ones screaming in shrill delight. Mindy's throat ached at the legs and arms pitched at puppyish angles. She wished she longed to dive onto the pile, to have grass in her nose, elbows in her ribs, but she didn't. She scooped up Shannon and held her tight.

"Down," Shannon whined, pushing at Mindy's ribs.

"I Amalia," the woman huffed as she climbed to her feet and shyly extended her hand. "I live," she pointed across the street. "Neighbors. Josefina," she added, pointing to the little girl who now hung on her back, arms clasped around her neck. "You like beans?" Amalia asked.

Mindy remembered their earthy perfume as she lumped them into the trash. "Oh, they were from you? How thoughtful. Very much. Thank you. Yes. Delicious." Mindy was aware of speaking gibberish, but wasn't sure if the woman could tell, and she might not even be listening, for Amalia had thrown herself on the grass and was hugging Josefina, smacking kisses along her neck as the girl squealed and squirmed.

Now Mindy perched at Clancy's busy bar, while Chris—necktie firm, hair in place—listed his reasons. "Not responsible" was one thing. "Not normal" was another. "For the child. Divorce." Mindy silently agreed, distracted by the constellations of twinkling lights in the row of potted topiary behind him. She watched Chris smile grimly at the waitress who left the bill. A hank of hair fell over his eyes as he signed his name on the credit slip.

· · · · ·

Mindy pulled into the underground employee parking lot through a sidewalk filled with pedestrians. That was odd. And Mindy was first to arrive: odder still. She punched the elevator button and tucked her sunglasses into her tote. Had she missed a memo? Was there an off-site meeting of which she was unaware? (She was afraid of losing her job.

She was afraid they were talking about her.) She averted her eyes from the mirrored doors, looking up only after they slid open and she stepped into the wood-paneled lobby. "Help you?" An unfamiliar security guard slouched at the console, watching a small television, where faint human shapes moved in a blizzard of static.

"No, thanks. Where's Jorge?"

"Probably washing his car." He smiled, revealing a gold tooth. "Jorge don't work weekends."

Mindy steadied herself with one hand on the cool marble counter. "I see." She rode the elevator to her office, sat in her chair, and laid her head down on her desk. The weekend loomed ahead without structure: a bridge with no span, a ladder without rungs. After a while she returned to the parking structure and sat in the dark in her car, looking into her crosshatched palms, feeling vaguely simian. Mindy revved the engine and spiraled back up the ramp, into the sun, the heat, the blasted Saturday. Traffic clogged the avenue. She merged homeward into the crush.

······

Sunday morning after Clancy's, Chris handed Mindy a sheaf of papers. "All you need to do is sign," he said. While he was in the shower, Mindy watched Shannon play in her netted pen. She tried to memorize the girl—the fruity burst of her skin, the depth of light in her eyes—and decided upon one last event.

Mindy strapped Shannon into her car seat and headed across town to the zoo. Shannon petted and sang to the elephant-shaped stroller Mindy pushed down winding paths under tall eucalyptus. Together they hooted at nervous monkeys, roared at the hind legs of sleeping lions, barked at the bristled whiskers of seals. They laughed with pink tongues at Shannon's first taste of cotton candy, and when they arrived home, the girl skipped across the lawn trumpeting all the animal sounds she could remember. Mindy grasped Shannon's arms and spun her around in a circle so her legs flew up from the ground. "Fly away! You're a bird," Mindy screamed, and Shannon screamed along with her, both of them crumpling to the ground. It wasn't until Chris came out, saying, "What have you done?" that Mindy noticed the girl was whimpering, in tears.

"My arms, my arms," Shannon cried. Mindy kissed Shannon and handed her to Chris. Shannon looked at Mindy over his shoulder, eyes narrowed, accusing, tired.

· · · · ·

When Mindy arrived home, a man in black waited at her doorstep. Mindy hesitated before getting out of the car. (She was afraid of Jehovah's Witnesses. She was afraid of rogue salesmen.)

The man waved. "Hallo. I am electrician. Landlord send." His thick accent flicked the "el" sounds up against his palate. He bowed slightly and retreated from the porch, stepping back onto the patch of gravel, taking care not to knock any plants or flowers. He seemed to be seven feet tall and stood hunched, as though he were used to stooping down to talk to people or to walk through doorways.

"No one told me you were coming," she said, passing by him to unlock the door. "I hope you weren't waiting long."

His black denim shirt and pegged jeans were freshly pressed. "I am just arrive," he said. "No problem." His dark leather shoes and belt were narrow and shone from lemon-scented polish.

She stepped into the foyer, dropped her bag, and continued down the hall to the haunted light switch. "This is it," she said, then turned to find no one there. The phone rang. Twice. Three times. The machine picked up, and Mindy returned to the front door, where the electrician was still outside, wiping his feet slowly, carefully, on the mat, waiting for a sign from Mindy to enter. None of that over friendly California casual crap.

"Please come in," she said, inspecting him as he ducked his head and stepped lightly inside. With his small wire-rim glasses, brushy gray halo of hair, and walrus-style mustache, he seemed to be a professor or intellectual of some sort. He stood in the middle of the small room with dark rings under his eyes; sunken cheekbones; large bony hands clasped calmly at his waist.

Valerie's voice blasted from the answering machine. "Yes, I know it's late notice, but you never have plans on a Saturday night, and it's time you quit playing the hermit. Dave's friend Harold is in from Chicago, and I'd, *we'd*, love you to come out with us. Nothing formal. Please say yes. Reservations at eight. Call me."

"I think there's a ghost in my light switch." Mindy felt ridiculous as she said it, inexplicably smoothing her hair and tossing it over her shoulder as she overexplained her problem with impromptu nocturnal illuminations. The electrician listened intently and did not respond as soon as she stopped speaking, which made her nervous, so she continued. "It might be dangerous, yes?" She blushed, realizing she had phrased her statement as a question so it might sound European. "Or maybe it's just me."

The electrician looked at her thoughtfully. He placed a crocheted mat on top of her dresser, then unwound his tool belt and placed that on the mat. "Life is dangerous," he replied, in a soft monotone.

"Yes, it is," Mindy agreed, while erasing Valerie's message. There was no way she was going out tonight after she had gone to work on a Saturday by mistake. "May I ask your name?"

"Vladimir." He hummed quietly while he unscrewed the switch plate, then tested the current with a small device. "Problem is here," he reported. "Not in you." He removed the gray metal mounting box from inside the wall and replaced it with a new one. He tested the current again, covered the box with a new switch plate, then swept up bits of dust and stray screws, cupping them in his hand, as though he were prepared to carry them outside Mindy's house.

Mindy made a bowl of her palms. "Please."

Vladimir smelled of warm starch as he leaned in to pour the bits of debris into her hands. "Exorcism complete," he proclaimed. "I demonstrate." The hall light went on when he toggled the switch one way, then off when he toggled it back. He replaced his screwdriver and the device into his tool kit, then rolled up the lace mat.

Mindy reached for her checkbook, but he clucked and shook his head. "Landlord will pay." He bowed slightly, his lavender-veined hand still poised midair.

She wasn't ready for him to leave. "Are you new to Los Angeles?"

"Like baby every day." He gave no indication of amusement or irony.

"Do you have family here?"

"Family, yes. Here, no." His hand suddenly closed and disappeared into his pocket. "Family is home. In Ukraine."

"Will they join you?" Mindy's hand was growing clammy and gritty. A sharp edge of metal bit into her palm.

Vladimir pulled his wallet from his back pocket and extracted a creased photo from the black leather fold. He stared at the photo, not sharing it with her. "I am dissident there. Not sure how to say. Maladapt. They want me to change something I believe in my bones. I must leave so my family can live. In here." He thumped his chest with his fist, a white bird slamming into a wall.

"Aren't you sad?" Mindy's heart beat fast.

"Of course!" he said fiercely. His yellow teeth appeared at odd angles, like a bouquet of old, twisted piano keys. "Every day. I think of them and they are here." He pointed to his head, casting a long shadow on the adjacent wall.

"Time. Reality." Vladimir spoke softly. "Is all construct." He was heading for the door now, shaking his head. He turned back to her. "You cannot forget—" Vladimir pulled an imaginary thread across a horizon, "—you can only live. Is only how I know to be free." He bowed. "I hope you will enjoy your dinner." Then he left.

Mindy threw herself onto her bed, lungs trembling, as if some small cataclysm waited there. A familiar chattering erupted outside, and when Mindy drew back the blanket from the window, it came off the wall in her hands. Mr. Owl clutched a mouse—still squealing!—in his horny talons. He ripped at it with his hooked beak, tore off a strip, and swallowed it in one great gulp. Mrs. Owl poked her head between his feet, tugging her own strip of flesh. Mindy wondered what attracted one owl to another, what made them a pair. She wondered if they'd ever had a little owlet, if that had changed their relationship or if they just took it all in stride in their parliament. Once they had devoured the mouse, they preened and primped, then rested against each other, motionless as bookends.

GARDENLAND

. . . . .

The silver dress was perfect. It showed off Chichi's still fine tits and camo'd the spray of blue veins above the backs of her knees. She turned off the overhead light and lit some candles, then sat on the closed the lid of the toilet just like her mother used to do. She'd been thinking a lot about her mother. Candlelight rippled against the turquoise and lavender tiles, transforming the small Spanish-style bathroom into a kind of nighttime aquarium. She inhaled the last of the lines from her hand mirror, then propped it up to start on her eyes. The phone rang and she only half-listened as Phil left a slurred message. "Baby, you almost ready? You're over an hour late and everyone's already sloshed. I know you don't want to miss your favorite bubbly on your big five-oh. You must be on your way. I'll try the cell."

Chichi's body had always been dynamite, but her eyes, she knew, were her best feature. It took more time to cover the lines now, more glitter to bring out the sparkle of her faded blues. Phil was a darling. Getting their friends together, renting the room, calling in favors to get a case of her favorite champagne. Her official birthday wasn't until Sunday but tonight, Friday night, was her party. Fifty fucking years old, twenty-five since she'd seen her mama. Chichi wondered what that might be like.

She imagined a garden hose coiled under a dripping faucet, its line of hissing spray snaked across a patch of rusty summer lawn. White plastic porch furniture, one chair pulled away, perfect for lounging on a Sacramento night. Mama would be turned out in a yellow sweater set and slacks, hair washed and feet bare, toes painted coral. She'd hold a glass of lemonade in one hand, a bowl of sugar in the other; and when she saw Chichi she'd likely let loose a scream. The lemonade might spill and the sugar bowl drop. They'd bend down to clean it up together, laughing over the sweet, sticky mess. After not seeing each other for so long, there would be words—of course there would be words. Only Chichi could never imagine them. She never pictured the inside of her mama's house either, only its flat beige exterior, soothing and dull. Suddenly, she had to go back. She knew if she didn't do it now, before the champagne hit, she never would

Dear Phil, she thought, *I am sorry, but I am going to miss my own party.*

Chichi packed a small bag. She wouldn't take much, but she needed a gift. Mama deserved something after all this time. In the place of honor on Chichi's stereo cabinet, under the light, was a tiny gold crown in a glass cube, dotted with jade and ruby chips. A gift from Phil after he took photos of her the first time. He was driving her back to her apartment in his green Gran Torino when they stopped at Norm's for fried eggs and pie. His swimming pool eyes promised her so many things: her photo on calendars, postcards, placemats, refrigerator magnets, magazine spreads, some of which had mostly come true. "From Thailand," Phil said when he placed the crown in her hands, and the newly-legal Chichi had thrilled at the exotic link. After they finished the pie, he drove her to the university campus, where they parked on the top level of Structure B to gaze at the goldfish sunset. She took off her shirt and Phil took more photos of her right there in his car. He screeched like a predatory bird when he came.

Chichi wrapped the crown in a clean dishtowel, stowed it in her bag, and took a good look around her apartment. No matter what happens, she thought, when I come back, everything will be different. She didn't even bother to change her clothes.

· · · · ·

Chichi sat across from Marilyn Monroe's lipstick-smudged drawer at Westwood Village Memorial Cemetery, her yearly ritual around the day of their birth, June first. A threesome of crows landed on the lawn near her feet. They cawed loudly, heaving breasts so black they pearled platinum in the moonlight. One brazen little fuck hopped close to peck at Chichi's brown paper sack. Chichi took the bottle of wine from the sack, screwed open the cap, and tossed back a ladylike slug. She held the wine in her mouth as she flattened the wrinkles from the brown paper and searched for a pen at the bottom of her purse.

Dear MM: My Big Five-Oh. Can you believe it? Ditching my own party. I love it. I doubt the fools will even miss me. As for last year's promises, I haven't done a line in over three months until tonight but if I hadn't, I wouldn't have realized I spent half my life away from home and now it's time to go back. I'd be lying if I said I wasn't twitchy about it—you never know what that woman might do when she sees me. And who knows what the hell I'll say to her. But this is my dream. You always tried to be true to yours, no matter how hard the world came down on you. I think of you, my inspiration, and how much we're the same, just always needing more love. Eternally yours, C.

Chichi reread the letter a few times to herself, pretending one time to be Marilyn and finding herself touched and pleased once she scratched out the last line, which she decided was too obvious and sad. Then she rolled the paper up into a ball, lit a cigarette and watched the words sink into themselves and disappear.

■ ■ ■ ■ ■

Chichi loved driving up the long deserted interstate and let her silver-blonde hair whip out the side window like a horse's tail. She found herself lost in sensual reveries—the mix of fear and excitement when she went home with strange men, getting mugged at knife point one night in Hollywood, the sound of her pinky finger snapping when she had to break into her own apartment—only to wake up, suddenly alert and driving. She was amazed when this happened, that she managed to stay inside the lines and not plow into anyone while her mind was so far away. She wondered how her mama really was, certain the sweater set/sugar bowl fantasy was only that.

Chichi had called home over the years just to hear her mama's voice. She called at different times of day to gauge the drinking. From different phones—pay phones at laundromats, mobile phones, house phones at parties of people she hardly knew—to make sure her mama wouldn't block the calls. Usually Chichi hung up right after "Hello," but sometimes she waited, listening to her mama's breath, or her long snapping inhale on a Newport. Sometimes she listened to the background TV, hysterical sitcom laughter or the screak of game show applause. Once her mama must have forgot to hang up or the receiver slipped from the cradle or the cell phone button didn't get pushed the right way. Chichi fell asleep listening to her mama's sighs, an occasional grunt as she heaved up or down into the sofa, the click-clack of a dog's toenails on linoleum, crackling candy bar wrappers.

Chichi's nerves jangled as soon as she hit the stretch of the interstate where the 5, 99 and 16 became one. She gripped the steering wheel as she crossed over Discovery Park, with its new duck-filled river—which was just an old cement drainage canal when she was a girl—and thickets of fresh trees. To the east, downtown Sacramento's skyline was a length of amber lights, much vaster than she'd ever seen. But as soon as she exited onto the El Camino Road, everything in the old Gardenland neighborhood looked just as Chichi remembered. Small houses sat far back from the street with long lawns and tall trees, some thick with fruit, surrounded by strict cyclone fences.

Mama's block was quiet and Chichi cut the engine before pulling up in front of her place. The beige house matched the dead lawn. Chichi started to get out of the car, but caught herself. She couldn't go knocking on Mama's door at two o'clock in the morning. Instinctively, Chichi made her way to the local main drag, now a wide boulevard almost unrecognizable. She'd stop for a bite, some coffee, maybe a line. She passed one chain restaurant after another as she drove through the Gateway Plaza, a new Gardenland development among many, until she came to a small one-story place at a back corner location. The Wagon Wheel diner, where she and her ex-husband Vince used to devour post-party pancakes at 3 a.m., advertised wine spritzer margaritas. A furnace of butterflies burned in Chichi's stomach as she steered her car towards the wooden arrow. The trees in the parking lot had been spindly and new back in the day. Now, the sallow green of their scant canopy and tumor-knobbed trunks left her feeling unmoored. She crossed the asphalt as though she were entering a memory that wasn't fully her own.

The bell tinkled on the heavy glass door and her silver sandals made sharp, tearing sounds on the sticky linoleum. The place was deserted. Chichi headed toward the back, past a long bank of windows covered with dark film that cast a milky purple glow on the orange booths and amber panes of glass that divided them. As she pushed open the door under the sign that said "Gals," a woman's husky laugh burst from the kitchen.

Chichi washed her hands and studied the mirror. She checked out her profile, her ass, adjusted her tits, smoothed her silver dress. Having lived half her life in Los Angeles, she had developed a certain city style, and would never be considered a gal. When Chichi came out of the ladies room, the hostess was waiting.

"Sorry 'bout that. Had my hands full," she said, straightening her hair and winking at someone over Chichi's shoulder. "Let's get you seated. Would you like to sit at the counter? Or I have this table over here."

Chichi studied the back of the woman as she followed her into the diner. Good curves, fair skin, a fresh piece of gum by the looks of her hard-working jaw. Younger than Chichi, but not as sexy. No fuckin' way. "I'll take this booth," Chichi said, slipping into one in the middle of the room.

"No can do. Booths are reserved for parties of four," the gal chirped.

"Are you shitting me?" Chichi looked around, still the only customer. "Your shirt's on inside-out."

A man's voice snorted behind the open kitchen counter as the hostess inspected her side seams and looked down the front of her blouse. "Oh my goodness," she said. "I was in such a rush…"

"Whatever." Chichi opened the menu, then without reading it, flung it back at the hostess. "Give me a half-stack of silver dollars, with strawberry syrup, not maple, lots of butter, skip the sugar, three strips of bacon, hot coffee and cold O.J." She could recite it in her sleep, and occasionally did.

The hostess took Chichi's ticket back to the counter and said something in a low voice. The man laughed louder this time, a familiar deep chuckle.

"Who's the laugher?" Chichi asked when the hostess came back with her coffee.

"Our Executive Chef is going to whip up something special just for you." Her smile suggested she knew what she was talking about.

Chichi dumped three packets of NutraSweet in her cup—two more than she normally took. She sensed him with her entire body, every hair on alert from the back of her neck to the V of her crotch, sensation flooding her brain, her brain reeling with the light and rush of him. Her hands clenched into fists, rough-bitten nails digging into her palms. Executive Chef at the friggin' Wagon Wheel. Jesus H.

The first time he came to her house to ask her out, she slammed the door in his face with a death threat. But their first date, God that car—white leather seats and a stampeding engine, burning donut rings in the parking lot at the shopping mall with her hands between his legs and her tongue in his ear. She swore she'd never marry him no matter how much he begged, but he begged just enough and she surrendered. He was an animal, her species, and she became one when she was with him.

He laughed as he helped the hostess take off her blouse to turn it the right way out, then murmured in that way that he had. Chichi pricked her ears to hear that piece-of-shit's voice—the croon of meaningless promises that flew like swallows from his red velvet tongue. She'd done her time chasing after those birds, holding crumbs in her open hands while they hopped this way and that.

When Chichi looked up he was there, all of him and so much of him was so much the same. The impudent slope of his shoulders, the Gothic lettering on his faded black T-shirt, the way he stood legs spread wide, like his nuts were too big to do else-wise.

"Well, looky here," he said. He tongued a toothpick from one corner of his cat's canary smile to the other, taking her in with his breath, with his thighs. "Patricia."

His hands seemed to sprout from the ends of his arms like heavy fruit. Amazing how delicate those huge hands could be. During the almost-year they were married, Chichi watched Vince thread needles to sew her name in his palm, clean pipe filters, roll scores of dollar bills for snorting and countless perfect joints. She'd get wet just watching the guy flick his Bic, shattered by the tiny orange flame cupped in his cavernous palm. She thought the divorce cured her, but here she was, practically jizzing her pants. She would say hello, she swore to God, that was all. But her hands drifted lazily above her head to drape her hair around both sides of her face, as though shaping an imminent embrace, lifting the low-cut part of her silver dress, as though Vince were a camera, her life spent in front of the lens insisting she find just the right trick of light, that she push one shoulder back just so. "I go by Chichi now," she drawled, willing herself not to say more, to refrain from one inviting word, one seductive gesture.

He slid into her booth and pushed her plate across the table. "Chichi. I like the sound of that. What you been up ta?" His smile was threatening and familiar.

Chichi drenched a forkful of pancakes in syrup, swirled it through the whipped butter, then raised the dripping fork to her lips. She closed her eyes and chewed slowly, humming at the sweetness in her mouth, promising herself, only Hello. Even then she could feel him raking her like a wolf on a flock of spring lambs. She knew how much he loved to watch her eat.

· · · · ·

"Place looks different," she said, looking around at his bachelor trailer.

"That's 'cause Pop ain't asleep in the corner," Vince nodded in the direction of the sagging easy chair propped in front of the small television. "He died about five years ago."

"I'm sorry," Chichi said. "Your pop was always nice to me."

"Boys were always nice to you." Vince laughed and bumped her with his hip, pushing her over onto his rumpled bed. "That was easy."

She felt instantly at home. "Honey, I was born easy."

"Except when we were married." He threw himself down next to her and cracked a couple cans of beer. "You look the same too," he said. "That teenage girl body with the porn star parts. That's some dress."

"Yeah, right," she said, sipping, privately pleased. "I look better in the dark."

"We'll see about that. Close your eyes."

She shivered as he pushed up her dress; she knew what was next. His lips took a wayward path down her stomach. "Tell me what's been going on." His moist finger entered her mouth, rubbed her gums, then rubbed some more down inside her.

"Vince, I don't do that anymore," she murmured, but already she liked where she was headed.

"Don't do what?"

He rubbed more powder on her lips, worked his hand like a bird. Fluttering, flying. She remembered now, what it was like to be with him, comforting as a bruise, convincing as a slap. Her legs scissored like chopsticks. "Fuck, Vince!" she cried.

"That's my girl!" He laughed and wrapped her legs behind him. "You want it. Tell me."

"I want it," she said, wondering how she remembered the words, the position. She was born this way. Born from him. "Of course I want it." Floating around in her head was how she wanted it. Floating where the dead were not dead. It was only a matter of time before her thoughts eclipsed the light. So sad when all she ever wanted was light.

He slapped her belly. "Don't fall asleep on me, doll."

She opened her eyes and saw him looking up at her, framed between her legs. She guffawed. "You could be my baby. Just like that. You could."

"Don't get sick on me. I'll stop. I swear I'll stop."

"No. Don't do that." They'd been in his trailer ever since he clocked out. But tomorrow was her birthday, and Chichi was in Sacramento, and Vince was going with her to visit Mama. A girl could do worse, and she had.

"I'm hungry," he said. "We been in here for hours."

"Ever since you watched me eat breakfast." She grinned.

"I'll be back," he said, stepping into black slacks, buttoning up his bowling style shirt with the orange flames burning at the hem. "I need to make a quick run for beer, tacos, cigarettes..." He ticked off his fingers.

"I quit," she said.

"Good for you. Some flowers for your ma." He winked. "Somebody's birthday present."

As Chichi scraped hardened pizza crusts into the trash, her brain swam with visions like glittering coins. Vince could get her pictures on calendars and placemats, get her that magazine spread Phil had never been able to score. She hummed as she wiped down the fronts of the cabinet doors, folded blankets and sheets ringed with stains of God-knew-what, stowed dirty pots and pans in the miniature oven and shoved his dirty clothes under the bed, stubbornly ignoring the clock.

An hour passed, then two, then it was Saturday night. He must have run into some friends and lost track of time, she thought. She brought her duffel bag from her car and took an uncomfortably cramped shower, then put her silver party dress back on just to remind him of what he'd been missing. By the time she put up her hair and glued on her eyelashes, she was worried and itching for a smoke. When Chichi knocked on the window of the neighboring trailer, wouldn't you know the most beautiful man she'd ever seen would have to go and open the door.

· · · · ·

If motherfucker Vince had been at that party, he wouldn't have let her drive. He would have buckled Chichi in the front seat and driven home slow, the back way, where there were no lights, no cops, no time for illusions. But motherfucker Vince wasn't there, hadn't even returned from the convenience store yet. The night had belonged to Chichi and the beautiful man, except the beautiful man had gone back to the trailer park hours ago, and Chichi'd stayed with the smokehouse guy, the guy with the shit and the throaty laugh who made her feel meaningless and destructive the first time he flicked his tongue at her.

It was hours before Chichi realized she had no wheels, no way to get back to Vince's trailer. The smokehouse guy had disappeared too. There was a locked door with loud voices behind it, but Chichi didn't want to bother with that. Anyway, she was mostly sober. Rain was just beginning to spit down as she tiptoed to the curb, a shoe on each shoulder. Her mouth tasted of chalk and pizza and the night jiggled lightly around her as she deliberately forgot the guy's one-syllable name and ridiculously dainty hands. She looked at the cars parked up and down the street. Most Gardenlanders left their cars unlocked; the truck would be the easiest to steal.

She pulled the wires down from under the dash and crossed them like her brother taught her when she was fourteen. She was soaked by the time she settled behind the wheel; her silver dress was now a botch of pure black. She could do this. It was only two miles. How long could it take? Seventeen miles an hour—shit—seventeen divided by a mile times sixty. She laughed. At this rate, she'd make it there by yesterday. She turned on the radio. Something country. Steel guitar sounded like heart strings, motherfucker always said. Goddamn romantic.

The big Ford's engine rumbled to life. Alone on the road, Chichi made it to the light at the end of the block without forgetting to stop, its one cherry eye beaming like vampire blood or a piece of a broken heart. There. Fine. The windshield wipers slappity slapped a momentary clearing before her vision puddled with rain again. It was so beautiful and dark around her, she could almost hear the quiet town breathe, could feel the streets rise like a man's belly in sleep. Men's bellies were so beautiful, the dark trail of hairs curling up like moss from between their beautiful legs with their beautiful cocks, slappity slap. A car was honking behind her now. That was beautiful too: a message of love between two machines, a gesture of recognition in the dense black night. The car honked again and its impatient driver swerved around her to the left. Chichi looked for the light, the light, to tell her to go or to stay in beauty.

But there was no light, just darkness. Dark like the insides of your eyes. Dark like a blindfold. Dark like inside the bad closet. Dark like home in a country boy's steel-stringed heart. She dug in her purse for a cigarette, then laughed when she remembered she'd quit. Somewhere outside someone started to yell, and Chichi panicked, accelerating in a beautiful rush of speed and sound, drawn forward by magnets and inner strength, into the darkness, the beautiful dark. There was no way she could have seen him until he ran right in front of her, waving his arms, chasing who knows what, some demons? Black, darkling butterflies? It was as though he flew straight into her and she saw him only on impact, his beautiful bloodied face.

· · · · ·

You could scrub as hard as you wanted with that Fels Naptha granny-ass soap, wax paper wrapped, scent like a sharp stick up your nose—but it never lathered luxurious and creamy like Dove. Fels Naptha was the Brillo of soap, its lather a barking growl that removed your skin with the dirt.

Chichi washed her hands until they shone pink, then scoured her feet with a lather like broken cement. Skin sloughed off in yellow, calloused layers. She'd gone barefoot since she was practically twelve. But that was a long time ago. I may be an old bitch, she thought, but my feet are baby-soft.

She kindled up another handful of thin, unsatisfying grit and looked in the mirror. Her whole damn face was a map of her life. The stitch at the end of her left eyebrow. Always been a bump there since the cut got infected. Such a prominent ridged scar for such a small tear, and it pulled up her brow so she looked Chinese on one side. Vince used to call it her Mexican facelift, her Tijuana Tuck. But she hated her face now and didn't have the presence of mind to blame the cheap, ruined glass. She draped Vince's old Ronrico Rum T-shirt over it. She didn't want to study what she saw. Didn't want to know if she had changed or if what she had seen was true.

The boy could be alive. He could certainly be alive. It was hard to say if he jumped off the hood of her truck or if he slid off as she drove away. She wanted to go back. Had a whole argument with herself about it, arguing still as she pulled into the trailer park and saw Vince hadn't yet returned. But she won the argument and decided to stay. Or had she lost?

Her neck ached from snaking forward and back when she'd slammed on the brakes. But whiplash was for pussies. She'd survived worse. She was waiting for him now. Again. Still. Reading his Ronrico Rum T-shirt backwards as she brushed her teeth. Turned the shirt inside out and read it some more. muR ocirnoR. Sounded like *Murder, She Wrote*. The thought of murder made her shiver and she splashed her face with rank water. Five times. Twenty five. Every time new. Every time clean. But not clean enough. She lathered up again, up to her elbows, like fancy dress gloves you'd wear to a Cinderella ball. Wandered around the house in her Fels Naptha gloves, made of the finest Corinthian Lather. Shit, now *that* was funny. Hoped she'd remember it so she could tell Vince. She missed her Chablis, but she vowed to quit everything. Smoking. Wine. Vince. Waiting. She thought about just getting in her car and going on without him, but it was too long since she'd seen him, and what happened last night scared her.

She squeezed her eyes shut and pretended she was blind. Took two babyfresh steps to the left into the crumbly foam mattress. Right, right. This was easy. Two steps forward and she was in the kitchenette. Yes, yes.

She stood at the small sink in her long, lather gloves, posing like Marilyn. One hand shading the Chinese eye like that photographer taught her, the other poised at the end of her long, graceful arm, waiting for a glass of Chablis, not champagne.

"Hey doll." It was Vince. He'd come in quiet like summer, his voice soft rain and crickets, delicious tobacco in the wreath of his hair.

"Shit! You scared me!" Her hand fell to her side, a bright autumn leaf.

"I brought flowers," he said, as he took down a cookie jar shaped like a pig. "You cleaned up." He kissed her cheek. "A woman's touch sure makes a difference."

Chichi took three steps sideways into the dinette, lost in her reverie, wondering how to correct the spin. When his eyes met hers, she would turn her hand over and present him her palm, like a kitten's belly. He'd fall for it and she'd surprise him with a quick slap. She wanted to see the print of her hand on his face, the quick hurt surprise in his eyes, yes, the hurt always made her wet. She found a pack of cards, dealt herself a game of Solitaire. Just to keep her focused, impartial.

Vince filled the jar with water, toweled off the drips, fluffed the daisies, and set them in the center of the small table before he pulled two packs of cigarettes from his pocket. He stripped one of its plastic, ripped open the foil interior with his teeth, and offered her one.

She leaned forward and touched her hand lightly to his as he cupped the match. "I slept with Shammi last night. Accidentally." So matter of fact, as though he'd said *I'll be back.*

"What do you mean accidentally? Did you drive into her?" Chichi inhaled half the cigarette, felt its nicotine treat blast her brain, fuel her heart. Fuck quitting. She watched the blossoming ash, the paper blackening and crackling behind it. She embroidered her name in the air with smoke, dotted the I's with two stabs of her fingers. She promised to quit everything again later, just not now.

"You know what I mean." He dropped his lazy lids over eyes the color of kerosene. "Let's not have no dogfight about it."

Chichi pretended to study the cards. The Queen of Hearts was about to get it on with the King of Spades. Big deal. Vince had sex with the ex. Chichi was the ex, too. And he was here now, right? With her, dig? They smoked together silently.

Finally Vince ground his filter onto the ceramic pig, then stood up to shrug off his powder blue jacket. He winged his arms out of his webbed suspenders, letting them hang down from his waistband like garters. He kicked off his blue and white loafers, peeled off shiny nylon socks, then rolled up the cuff of his matching powder blue pants.

Chichi slid the queen to her queen. "Weren't you wearing something else when you left?"

"Yes, ma'am. Shammi felt like doing a little shopping." He plopped down on the foam cushion next to her, wriggling his toes in the air. "You like?"

She looked him up and down, as though noticing him for the very first time, which she wasn't but it felt like that anyway, except they weren't in The Wagon Wheel where everything started. Again. They were in Gardenland Mobile Home & RV Park. "You look like the frigging Easter pimp."

"The what?" His head swiveled at her. His eyes bulged and his mouth hung open. She could see his gold molars in the back, all five. Money in the bank, he called them.

"You heard me," she said, finally pulling the seven that was the key to the game, to everything, one card slapping quickly on top of another now, four little piles triumphant at the top of the table, slap, slap, slap, slap! Royalty, one after the other.

"Why you don't got no clothes on?" he asked, lolling back on the futon, crooking his pinky at her and patting the space next to him, lazing that enchilada hand of his all along his crotch.

Chichi lit a new cigarette off her old one, then balanced it on the edge of the table where she hoped it would melt the ugly Formica top, maybe torch the whole freakin' trailer park. She lay down next to Vince, tears in her eyes. She would tell him about the accident, but first she had to get him ready. She opened her mouth and he kissed her.

"I'm not feeling it, doll."

She ground into him rhythmically.

She.

Would.

Tell.

Him.

But not now. Tomorrow. Soon. What did it matter when, if they were going to be together for eternity?

· · · · ·

Sunday. Chichi's Big Five-Oh. She could hardly believe it. Vince gave her a hell of a good-morning screw, but didn't seem to be in any big hurry to get on the road to Mama's. When he lit out for cigarettes yet again, Chichi packed up her bag, got in her car and drove back to the place where it happened. She went during daylight, on her big day. Somehow it felt braver, like more of a punishment. She sat on the curb and smoked until the cigarettes were gone, then cried until her feet were damp with tears. A couple of teenage boys stood right where it happened, as though the dead or maybe not dead boy had melted into the soil and from his mess had sprung two brand-new boys. They wore crew necks, long shorts like skirts, and knee-high athletic socks. Must be some kind of a church made them dress that way. There was one skateboard between them, and they alternated throwing it down on the street, hopping on it, and falling onto a patch of dried grass. One of them spray-painted something on the long cinder block wall, pointed at Chichi and laughed. BITH, he had written, in voluptuous pussy-pink letters. The boys laughed like dogs and ran down the street, pushing each other into walls, bushes, parked cars. "You spelled it wrong, peckerheads," Chichi yelled after them.

She stood and brushed off her bottom, which ached from her long sit on cement. She kicked off her flip-flops and clomped barefoot to an abandoned gas station. She squeezed through a slash in the chain-link fence and headed toward the back of the small outbuilding, where a massive tropical vine had taken root and grown wild. Fuchsia blooms as big as her fists covered one wall up to the roof. An insane chirping came from somewhere below. Baby birds, throats open, gasping and calling. It made her sick.

It was close to lunchtime now. Her mama was probably asleep. There was still time—there was still the whole rest of her day—so Chichi went back to the trailer to wait. She sat on the little square porch, her purse on her lap, peeling off the flakes of green paint from the concrete pad that was supposed to be a patio, possibly a lanai. She'd tell off the bastard, then leave, with or without him. She hoped with. What if it was all a dream anyway? What if everything was meaningless? And we were just plastic zoo animals and our words were alphabet magnets.

She dug to the bottom of her purse. There was this one picture of her where she looked like a movie star, she really fucking did, and she automatically thought of Marilyn, the way her toe pointed, the shine on her cheek, biting her scarf. There used to be lots of photos of Chichi like that, but now there was only the one, dog-eared at the corners and burned a bit where she'd dozed off smoking while looking at it as she did from time to time. It wasn't her favorite; she'd always said the Lucite shoes took the spotlight away from her legs and you could almost see the lines of her cooch, but still. Someday she ought to frame it.

THE POSSUM EFFECT

. . . . .

I walked down the stairs to the front door and found a baby possum with a black face scrabbling at the threshold, trying to get inside. When he finally realized he was not getting in without a key, he waddled down the path to the back of the house. I followed from a distance, then crouched down and saw his eyes like sequins in the shadows under the porch. I was happy when I went inside.

I called Carl at his office. "We are the proud parents of a black-faced baby possum."

"Great," he said. "Now we don't need to have a kid. What should we have for dinner?"

Over halibut with noodles in ponzu sauce, I continued to talk about the possum. I talked about how it might like to sleep on my old wool sweater. I talked about feeding it last week's wrinkled kiwi fruit. Maybe even converting the old kitty condo into a postmodern possum condo. I named the possum Dixon.

"You named it?" Carl asked.

I said I thought I might be getting attached and hoped we could keep it.

Carl said it was best to leave the possum be as nature intended, and that the cat would get jealous if we adopted a possum.

We were the proud parents of a black-faced cat named Gary. Gary the cat made me feel fuzzy and vaguely domestic, while Dixon the possum made me feel connected to an untamed world of primal instinct.

I talked to Nancy the therapist about these feelings. She was all for renovating the condo and giving the possum the sweater and the kiwi. "Go for the joy," she said. Nancy gets my subtext.

Like when I told her about meeting Carl for the first time and experiencing an extraordinary push/pull phenomenon. One giant invisible hand pushed me closer to him, another one pulled me away. Nancy said, "Decide which hand is the hand of fear, then don't listen to it." Luckily, the push hand won out. Now, whenever I get a bit mental from the effects of the push/pull phenomenon, Carl puts his hand—neither giant nor invisible—on my shoulder and says, "Let me be your grounding pole," and everything is instantly okay.

When I told Carl what Nancy said about going for the joy with Dixon, he said, "Do you really think you're going to have time to take care of a wild animal every day?"

We did have a lot going on in our lives. It was already a bother to feed Gary the cat—whom we loved dearly—and to keep her box properly scooped up. There were tons of things Carl and I planned on doing—like writing stories and walking the pilgrim's trail to Santiago de Compostela—that made raising a baby possum difficult to accommodate. I didn't say anything.

Carl raised his eyebrows at me as if I needed a grounding pole. "What are we now? *Married with Children?*"

Actually, one reason we got along so well was because we weren't anything like *Married with Children*. It's important to know at the beginning which sitcom title best applies to your relationship, and we both had always known that one didn't.

The next day, I had this underground idea to stop by a pet store and do some research on how to care for possums, or maybe pick up materials for renovating Gary the cat's condo. I wanted to feel I was doing something to make the possum feel safe. As Carl and I were heading out to the Farmer's Market to shop for butternut squash and Swiss chard, I said, "Let's go see if Dixon still lives under the porch." I admit it: I was hoping the possum's ratty black face would seduce Carl like it had seduced me, and that Carl would have to consider changing his life just a bit to include it.

When we went into the backyard, Dixon had been decapitated. His head was lying six inches from a pile of guts and a thatch of fur. The sun was hot. Flies were buzzing. Gary the cat had followed us and was blindly stepping in visceral goo. I wondered a whole lot of things at once. Why hadn't I gone out possum condo shopping sooner? Why had it taken so long for me to act on my maternal instincts? And what kind of predator could have launched such a gruesome crusade? Possums and sparrows, skunks and squirrels had been romping wildly through our yard for years and the cat had never batted an eyelid, which was why I often thought of Gary as "The Ambassador of Peace." Bad dogs wandered in now and again, but they always made lots of noise and we hadn't heard anything. "Ew. Well," I said. "The world really is one big issue of *National Geographic*, isn't it?"

"Pretty much," Carl said, and set about cleaning up the mess.

I wish I could say I threw myself on the bed and beat my breast with sorrow, but I didn't. We were sad when we went to the Farmer's Market. Quiet while we rinsed the chard and scooped out the squash. The few people I told about the possum, I had to un-tell.

The next day, as Carl and I were leaving to go for a walk, there was a crashing in the elephant fern out front. I saw a rat-tail bottom, then a *white-faced* baby possum, slowly burrowing under our fence and into the neighbor's yard. This one didn't even come near our front door. Maybe it would survive. I felt better. Thoughts of condos and kiwi fruit never even entered my head. I had changed from being a person who wanted to care for something small and wild, to a person who knew that it wouldn't work out. But I still hadn't figured out how to go for my joy, and obviously didn't have it in me to care for a life. This made me feel crappy again, so I went online to start planning a trip to Spain. That's when I learned that "Santiago de Compostela" translated to "St. James in a Field of Stars." How gorgeous is that? I also learned that Saint James was decapitated by King Herod himself, after which his body was taken up by angels. His head too, I guess. I started to feel better again and thought maybe it was time to write a story, which always made me feel like I was going for my joy.

A few days later, Carl told me he was working on a new story. It was about a couple whose child has died. Their grieving cycle is on the mend when the wife discovers a possum in the backyard, which she becomes quite fond of. The husband is happy because it's the first time she's been excited about anything for a long time. They have some decent sex. The wife talks to her therapist about the possum. The therapist tells the wife to go for the joy, but when the wife suggests turning the possum into a pet, the husband pooh-poohs the idea. When the possum is killed, the husband wishes he had supported his wife's desire to turn the possum into a pet.

Carl's synopsis wasn't entirely surprising. We both had a tendency to cannibalize our personal lives and distasteful inner whatnot for the sake of a story. Plus, I got Carl's subtext. He, too, experienced the invisible hand of fear, especially when it came to *Married with Children*. "What's the wife's name?" I asked.

"Barbara."

"Regular Barbara, or Streisand Barbra?"

"Regular. Three As."

That was a relief. "You're not worried about our sex life, are you?" What with the decapitation and all, sex had sort of fallen off the schedule.

"Ask me later tonight."

I smiled. "I like your story," I said. "But it's only got two things. You need three things for story magic."

"Says who?"

"I don't know," I said, "I think I read it somewhere."

"Huh," he said. "I wasn't going to tell you about the story."

I told him I thought it was good that he did. If it had been published and I had suddenly read about his personal life with some woman named Barbara, I would have been annoyed. Anyway, I added, the only people who shouldn't see stories are mothers. All the reading between the lines really complicates holidays. Then I told him my theory about Gary being the Ambassador of Peace. He was amused and later used the grounding pole effect to revitalize our sex life.

I had fiction workshop the next night, and got home pretty late. Carl was sitting on the couch with the cat. "How was your day?" I asked.

"Pretty good," he said. "I wrote another thing into the story. The wife is so sad after the death of the black-faced possum, that when the husband sees the white-faced possum, he renovates the kitty condo so his wife can take care of it if she wants to."

"Genius," I said. "Guess what I wrote about?"

He started to laugh, which made me laugh, which made him put his hand on my leg, which started the grounding pole effect, which made me fall into his lap, and we stayed like that for a long time, petting the Ambassador and talking about how people usually get exactly what they want, even if sometimes they don't always know that they want it.

ACKNOWLEDGMENTS

. . . . .

Grateful acknowledgments to the editors of the following publications in which these stories first appeared, as well as to Subito Press (University of Boulder, Colorado), which published them as a collection (*Moon Is Cotton & She Laugh All Night*, 2010): "Glossolalia" in *Whiskey Island Magazine*; "Superbaby Saves Slugville" in *North Dakota Quarterly*; "Troglodyte" in *New South*; "Call It a Hat" in *The Pinch* and in the anthology *Art From Art*; and "Gardenland" in *Another Chicago Magazine*.

Additional gratitude to these editors for publishing these stories: "Xmas of Love" in the anthology *First Light: Poems, Stories and Essays of the Winter Holiday Season*; 2011 Tusculum Review Prize Winner "Badass" in *The Tusculum Review*; "Help Me Find My Killer" in *Elixir*; "Gneiss" in *Quiddity: International Literary Journal and Public-Radio Program*; "Spontaneous Light" in *Phantasmagoria*; and "The Possum Effect" (formerly titled "National Geographic") in *Rio Grande Review* and *Be Which* magazine.

TITLES FROM ELIXIR PRESS

. . . . .

Perpetual Care by Katie Cappello

The Raindrop's Gospel: The Trials of St. Jerome and St. Paula by Maurya Simon

Prelude to Air from Water by Sandy Florian

Let Me Open You A Swan by Deborah Bogen

Cargo by Kristin Kelly

Spit by Esther Lee

Rag & Bone by Kathryn Nuernberger

Kingdom of Throat-stuck Luck by George Kalamaras

Mormon Boy by Seth Brady Tucker

Nostalgia for the Criminal Past by Kathleen Winter

Little Oblivion by Susan Allspaw

Quelled Communiqués by Chloë Joan López

Stupor by David Ray Vance

FICTION

How Things Break by Kerala Goodkin

Nine Ten Again by Phil Condon

Memory Sickness by Phong Nguyen

Troglodyte by Tracy DeBrincat

LIMITED EDITION CHAPBOOKS

Juju by Judy Moffat

Grass by Sean Aden Lovelace

X-Testaments by Karen Zealand

Rapture by Sarah Kennedy

Green Ink Wings by Sherre Myers

Orange Reminds You Of Listening by Kristin Abraham

In What I Have Done & What I Have Failed To Do by Joseph P. Wood

Hymn of Ash by George Looney

Bray by Paul Gibbons